Ellora's Cave Publishing, Inc.

Ellora's Cave Publishing, Inc.
PO Box 787
Hudson, OH 44236-0787

ISBN # 1-84360-390-X

Edited by Martha Punches and Cris Brashear.
Cover art by Scott Carpenter.

Warning: The following material contains strong sexual content meant for mature readers. *Taken* has been rated NC17, erotic, by six independent reviewers. We strongly suggest storing this book in a place where young readers not meant to view it are unlikely to happen upon it. That said, enjoy…

TAKEN

Also by Jaid Black
(Trek Mi Q'an series)

- The Empress' New Clothes
- Seized
- No Mercy
- Enslaved
- No Escape
- Naughty Nancy (*Things That Go Bump In The Night* anthology)
- No Fear

Also by Joanna Wylde
(futuristic series)

- The Price Of Pleasure
- The Price Of Freedom
- The Price Of Power

Also by Shelby Morgen
(The Northlanders Volume 1 series)

- A Slave's Price
- A Rogue's Virtue
- A Sorcerer's Seduction
- A Warrior's Pride

Dementia
A Trek Mi Q'an Tale

Written by

Jaid Black

Chapter 1

The highlander jungle of planet Dementia
Star system of the third dimension

Her friends called her the Schemer, or Scheme for short, for she had always been well known for her ability to get out of tight situations. But as she ran through the dense Dementian jungle panting for air, her heartbeat drumming like mad against her chest, Delores Ellison was afraid that, for the very first time in her twenty-nine years, she had gotten herself into a situation there was no squeezing out of.

Her father had always said she was too much like her mother for his peace of mind. Perhaps he had been right.

Dee dashed through the overgrown jungle as fast as her feet would carry her. She ignored the rogue strands of golden hair that whipped into her eyes and stung them, and instead concentrated her energy on escaping the gorilla fighter whose hunting skills were proving to be frighteningly keen.

He's gaining on me, she thought hysterically as she braved a quick glance over her shoulder. *Good God in heaven, do not let this beast enslave me!*

She still didn't know how it had happened, still had no clue how she'd ever been catapulted from earth to this…this…place. But she had been in Dementia for over a year now, and, at least until this night of reckoning, had managed to thwart any would-be slave traders from capturing her.

She had survived on berries and an odd blue fish for sustenance, slept in hollowed out stone caves for protection from the elements, all the while searching in vain for the bizarre stone icon shaped like a gorilla's head that she had been holding when she'd been mystically transported to this dark, frightening world so reminiscent of *Planet of the Apes*. Dee was certain that if only she could find that talisman—or whatever in the hell it was—she could go back to earth, back to home.

She ran into the night, dashed through the highlander jungle terrain she had grown accustomed to, her breath coming out in short gasps. She knew—*knew*—that the gorilla fighter was gaining on her, would catch her at any moment if she didn't figure out a way to escape him. She could sense his sharp green eyes on her, could hear the low growl of a predator hissing in his throat…

Please, she silently begged the heavens. *I do not want to be a slave! Oh God—oh please God help me!*

Dee ran impossibly faster, ignoring the buzzing sound of the insect predators that swarmed throughout the dense terrain. She knew what those gorillas had done to that one human girl, the one she had tried to escape Dementia with six months ago. Knew too that the Dementian males coveted humanoid females as nothing more than sex slaves and serving girls.

The one tracking her now was called Zaab—General Zaab if she'd overheard the villagers of the Mantus Hoard correctly. Zaab had once been a lowlander lieutenant, but had taken over the highlander Mantus Hoard by force when its elderly leader was assassinated by fellow tribesmen. And so now the new general ruled with an iron fist, and in just under a year had made the Mantus the most respected—and feared—gorilla fighters on the planet.

Zaab. This wasn't the first time he had hunted Dee, not the first time he had attempted to enslave her. But, she thought as she ran faster and faster still, it might well be the last time he'd have to hunt her if she didn't figure a way out of this mess. Twice before he had stalked her, twice before she had thwarted him. The third time would prove to be a charm—but whether for her or for him…

Zaab.

He stood upright like a human, possessed the mental acuity of a human, and even carried the masculine scent of a human, yet this male was no human…

A gorilla. If she didn't get herself out of this situation, Dee thought in anguish as she struggled to breathe, then she would become the sex slave of a gorilla.

No.

The eerily moaning wind swarmed about her, crashing through the rough alien terrain. She could feel him getting close, then closer still, could sense his sharp, possessive eyes narrowed on her…

Run, Dee! Run!

Dee cried out softly in her throat as the low growling sound grew alarmingly closer. Her heartbeat was thumping like a rock against her chest, her blue eyes wide and her breathing labored. She made a quick left turn into the thickest portion of the jungle and dashed into it, knowing it was an unsafe place to be, but also realizing that if she was to thwart Zaab for a third time then this was the only way.

Help me! she mentally pleaded. *Dear God in heaven please help me!*

Dee screamed out when the sharp stinger of a predatorial vine shot through her thigh, effectively throwing her to the ground while it slowly drugged her with hallucinogen. She cried out again when the thick leafy tentacles entwined themselves around her limbs, the snappers instantly shredding what clothing she'd had on as they laid her out spread-eagle and naked on the jungle floor.

Not the vines – oh no, not the vines.

She knew it was over. Knew too that Zaab had won. If the general didn't track her down by scent, then the vines would have their wicked way with her, dining on her cunt juice until she died, dehydrated and mentally broken. Either way, it was over…

The vines were the method Dementians used to break human female slaves to their bidding. The predatorial plant would intravenously pump a euphoric hallucinogen into her system, making her orgasm over and over again, providing them with the juice they dined on, until she literally died of pleasure and dehydration. The hallucinogen would also drive her insane if given too much of it, insuring that the only way she'd ever again possess the mental wherewithal to leave Dementia was through death.

Dee cried out softly as two pink flower buds from the vine clamped onto her nipples and began suctioning at them. They stiffened immediately, causing her to moan. *It's over,* she thought, closing her eyes as the hallucinogen began to take effect. *It's all over…*

The sound of a low, arrogant growl filled her mind. She blinked slowly, opening her blue eyes on a moan as a third flower bud clamped onto her clit and began suctioning it. She shuddered, knowing an orgasm was imminent.

The general stood above her, his piercing green eyes flicking possessively over her naked, splayed out body. His gaze settled on her cunt and lingered there, then darted up the length of her to meet her eyes.

Zaab.

Dee swallowed roughly, wondering through the euphoric daze that was quickly engulfing her just how long it would take before she was begging the bastard to fuck her. A male in his prime, an alpha male who owned more slaves than she could count, would know very well—too well—how to use the vines to get what he wanted.

She groaned and simultaneously arched her hips as the first powerful orgasm hit. She closed her eyes tightly, not wanting to watch his expression, for she could sense his arrogant pleasure as though it was a tangible thing. He knew he'd won, knew too that he could do anything he wanted with her…

The rustling sound of discarded leather clothing induced her eyes to sleepily open for a moment. It was hard to focus on any one thing for the euphoria was hitting fast, but she was alert enough to recognize the naked, powerful Dementian male standing over her.

Zaab.

His body was at least seven feet tall—probably more. His musculature was extreme, without a doubt the most powerful and heavily muscled body she'd ever laid eyes on. Two deadly incisors jutted out from his otherwise human-looking teeth, a grim reminder that he could slice through her jugular like melted butter.

Her eyes flicked down to his stone-hard cock. She nervously wetted her lips, again wondering how long it would take before she was begging the general to fuck her.

And then the euphoria kicked in and she no longer cared.

Chapter 2

Surreality engulfed all of her senses. Her mind swam as if dreaming, or as if existing on another plane far removed from the cold jungle floor she lay naked and spread-eagle upon. She shuddered and moaned as the flower buds on the vines clamped down harder onto her erect nipples and swollen clit, her legs shaking as she violently climaxed. Again.

And still, the general made no move to fuck her.

She felt like she'd been coming for hours—days even. Yet realistically she knew it was the hallucinogen making her feel that way. No more than fifteen minutes could have passed by since the vines had snagged her, but the painfully hedonistic euphoria made the time seem endless.

She needed to be mounted. She needed to be fucked more than she needed to breathe.

Zaab was watching her, she knew. His piercing green eyes were evaluating and assessing her bodily responses with the acuity of a hawk, and yet he still hadn't bothered to touch her, let alone to impale her with his huge cock.

She gritted her teeth, refusing to beg. He knew what the vines were doing to her, realized that she would give anything—do anything—say anything—to be fucked over and over, again and again…

"How do you feel, lass?" he murmured, squatting down beside her on his powerful thighs. He ran a large, rough hand over her belly, then brought it up to cup one breast. Apparently irritated that the suctioning flower bud was in the way of his touching her nipple, he pulled it off, snapped the head, and threw that particular portion of the vine to the wayside. He ran his thumb over her nipple, making her gasp, then asked again, "How do you feel?"

Dee wetted her lips, trying to make eye contact but in too dreamy of a state to focus her attention. "I…I…tired," she whispered, closing her eyes again. "Frustrated." That small admission was as close to begging as she'd allow herself to sink.

"Tell me what you need," he murmured. She heard the other flower bud make a popping sound as it was forced from her other nipple. A second later that one was snapped too and two large Dementian hands settled in at her breasts and toyed with her nipples, making them ache so much more than the vines had.

"Please," she whimpered, her hips arching up as much as they could while being roped down to the ground with vines. "Make it stop." Another small admission, but one she couldn't seem to keep from making.

"Hmm," he purred noncommittally, his primal male face coming into her line of vision. His thumbs and forefingers plucked at her nipples, plumping them up.

She sucked in her breath and arched her hips as he settled himself intimately between her outspread thighs. He made no move to displace the flower bud sucking vigorously at her clit, opting instead to watch as she convulsed again from another orgasm the plant-mouth brought on.

"Please," she said more forcefully, refusing to allow her voice to quiver into a pleading sound. *"Please."*

Zaab ignored her. She gritted her teeth.

The general released her breasts and placed some bizarre, fleshy-looking contraption next to her body, a boxy device she'd never seen before. He removed the needle that the predatorial vine had shot into her thigh and momentarily disabled it by sticking the needled portion of it into the faux flesh-box.

So that was how he would keep the vine alive if he needed it again, she thought hesitantly. He was nobody's fool. He'd disallow the hallucinogen to kill her, but he'd also keep it handy if he needed to torture her into submission with the euphoria it generated.

Good God, she'd never escape him.

Not that the sexual euphoria she was already experiencing was even close to waning, she thought with near-hysteria. It seemed to grow worse and worse, making her want to clamp her legs together and squeeze, inducing her breathing to hitch and her pupils to dilate. "Please," she said pitifully, no longer caring if she begged or not. "Please help me."

Zaab purred at her submissive words, his warm palms running over her belly. "I've the feeling you will be worth the wait, lass," he murmured, those piercing green eyes straying down to her puffed up cunt. She knew he was referring to the other two times she'd escaped from him—before he could mount her.

With a growl, he pushed her thighs further apart, making her breathing hitch. From fright or anticipation she couldn't say. She laid spread out before him, her hands roped to the jungle floor above her head, her thighs tied down to the ground making movement—and escape—impossible.

"Please!" she said louder, more pleadingly, her splintered brain making the connection between begging and the promise of release. Her head thrashed from side to side as the flower bud sucking on her clit grew more suctioning. "Oh god...*I'm begging you!*"

"Mmmm," he growled, his incisors bared. He palmed his massive cock and placed the tip at the opening to her pussy. "That's a good girl," he said in a patronizingly agreeable tone. "Such a sweet, biddable, little wench..."

Her nostrils flared in renewed anger. Her jaw clenched as she narrowed her icy blue eyes at him.

Enraged at the insult, Zaab let out an ear-piercing bellow as he stared down at her, his acute green eyes narrowed in anger. She flinched when he pulled his cock away from her wet opening, then whimpered when he removed his hands from her breasts.

"I…I'm sorry!" she said truthfully, thrusting her hips up at him as best as she could. "I won't do that again—I swear!" Anything—she'd do anything if only he'd fuck her, she thought hysterically.

The low growl in Zaab's throat told her the subtle rejoinder hadn't been quite forgotten by the arrogant male. And if her guess was accurate, he was still smarting from more than her show of defiance—he was still reeling from the knowledge that a human female had managed to elude him for more than six months.

Sometimes, mostly when sleeping alone in the stone caves late at night, she had often wondered if they had become the other's phantom obsession.

Dee ground her hips in a wanton, carnal gesture. Her breasts heaved up and down in time with her labored breathing. Beads of perspiration covered her torso. She no longer cared how pathetic she looked, no longer cared that the unthinkable had happened and she had been captured by her nemesis. Later, there would be time to think on that. For now, all she wanted was to be mounted.

"I swear I'll be good," she said throatily, her hips grinding up as she submissively lowered her eyelashes. "Please help me."

He was snarling down at her, the predator in him obvious, but she could also see his nostrils flexing, telling her he couldn't resist indulging in the scent of her arousal. She took comfort in that, hoping he would forget his anger long enough to put her out of the euphoric misery.

The flower bud at her clit began suctioning more vigorously, making her gasp. Her back arched, lifting up her breasts like two offerings. *"Oh god."* Her head fell back on the jungle floor, her nipples stabbing upwards. She hesitated for the briefest of moments, then turned her head, baring her neck to him.

The vines tightened their hold on her thighs, pinioning her motionless while the flower bud suckled juice from her cunt. She gritted her teeth, not wanting to come again, for her juice only made the bud suck harder and faster.

She was going to go mad. She was going to die of pleasure.

"Ah, you have bared your neck to me, lass," Zaab murmured in that arrogant tone of his. The baring of one's neck was a gesture of submission amongst predator peoples and they both knew it. Where her words had meant little, apparently her actions meant a lot.

His palms came down to knead her aching breasts again, making her moan. His fingers flicked at the nipples, inducing her back to arch and her hips to flare up. "Please," she whispered, tears clouding her vision. She was going to go insane—if he didn't help her she knew her mind would grow splintered. "I...I..."

His face engulfed her line of vision, blocking out the low-hanging moons overhead. All she could see was Zaab and his sharp green eyes. "You what?" he purred, knowing how difficult it was for her to plead with him. "A good wench always tells her Master what He needs to hear."

She swallowed against the lump in her throat, throwing her hips up at him again, wanting to grind her pussy against his cock. "I beg you," she said softly, quietly—*pleadingly*. "I beg you to fuck me."

His nostrils flared at the precise moment she heard the low growl in his throat resume. She wet her lips, praying that meant what she thought it did.

Zaab thrust her thighs apart again, his nostrils inhaling her scent. "I beg you to fuck me…what?" he growled.

"Master," she breathed out, her breasts heaving upward, wanting him to knead them a bit more roughly. "I beg you to fuck me, Master."

"And will you beg your Master to fuck you every night, slave?" he asked, the head of his thick cock again settling at the opening of her pussy.

"Yes."

"I didn't hear you, lass."

"Yes."

"And will you beg my brothers to fuck you as well, slave?"

Dee hesitated, not knowing what the correct answer was. She'd never gotten close enough to the Dementians to be aware of what transpired behind closed hut doors. She knew only of the things that transpired in public places. "Only if it pleases the Master," she softly hedged.

He purred again, telling her she'd answered well enough. "Good girl." He grabbed her breasts roughly, his dagger-like incisors bared. "And for the record, wench, you are not permitted to *ever* fuck another."

Until he sold her to someone else? *Would* he sell her to someone else?

Did it matter?

Zaab used his powerful legs to spread her already splayed thighs further apart. Grabbing the flower bud at the head, he popped it off her clit and snapped it in two. "Do you understand me, lass?"

"Yes."

"I didn't hear you, slave."

She wanted to cry. "Yes!" The euphoria was maddening, horrific…

With a primitive growl, he thrust his huge cock inside of her enveloping flesh, impaling her cunt in one deep thrust. She could hear the suctioning sound her pussy made as he slowly pulled back and stroked out of her, as if her body was trying to pull his cock back in to the hilt.

"Oh god," she moaned, trying in vain to throw her hips at him the way she wanted to. She could see his teeth gritting, the vein at his neck bulging. She wanted him to thrust fast and deep inside of her. *"Oh god – please."*

Zaab gave her what she wanted, growling low in his throat as he plunged in and out of her cunt, over and over, again and again. He rode her hard, like an animal, impaling her enveloping flesh like a battering ram.

His silky black mane of hair tickled her breasts, running like silk over her nipples as he fucked her.

"Do you like this, slave?" he arrogantly ground out, the muscles in his arms bulging as he repeatedly buried his thick cock deep inside of her.

Dee's head thrashed from side to side, sexual euphoria overwhelming her. *"Yes."*

"Yes what?"

"Yes, Master."

He rewarded her obedient answer with harder, deeper strokes, threading her golden hair around one hand as his other hand kneaded her breasts and played with her nipples. He rode her body ruthlessly, going primal on her cunt, marking her flesh with his scent.

She closed her eyes on a moan, her hands tied above her head, her breasts jiggling, as the Alpha Male of the Mantus Hoard fucked her long and hard. She came over and over, again and again, moaning and groaning, marking him with her scent as much as he meant to mark her with his.

"Beg for my cum, slave," Zaab growled, his cock plunging into her flesh in fast strokes. "Beg your Master to mark you."

"Yes – please – Master..."

Dee's half delirious gaze clashed with his alert green one. She could see his jaw clenching, his nostrils flaring. Perversely, the knowledge that she was the cause of such a rigid, controlled male showing even that much emotion made her impossibly wetter.

Zaab lowered his face to her neck as he continued to mount her, a low, warning growl hissing low in his throat. She tensed, realizing as she did that he was displaying his dominance over her. He could slice through her jugular at any time, that growl resonating through her eardrum said. He could kill her, he could fuck her, he could enslave her...

Dee gasped when his incisors scraped against her jugular vein, fear causing her eyes to close tightly. He grunted, as if pleased she had at last realized who it was that held all power over her.

"Relax, lass," he purred near her ear as he stroked in and out of her cunt. "If you're a biddable little wench," he ground out, his thrusts coming faster and harder as he wrapped his hand more securely around her hair, "you will know my pleasure instead of my wrath."

He took her hard then—harder than ever before. His hips pistoned back and forth as he plunged his cock in and out of her suctioning flesh, his jaw clenched tightly as he drove them both toward orgasm.

"Yes," Dee groaned, unable to move, unable to do anything but lie there and feel him fucking her. *"Oh god."*

She came violently—convulsively, her loud moan echoing throughout the highlander alien jungle. *"Yes—oh god yes."* Her thighs shook like leaves in a storm as her head thrashed madly from side to side. She groaned when his thrusts became impossibly faster, more primal and animalistic.

"Who owns this cunt?" Zaab ground out, the fingers threaded through her hair clenching the strands tighter. *"Tell me."*

"Master!" Dee cried out, another violent orgasm crashing over her. "Master Zaab!"

He growled low in his throat as he stiffened above her, thrusting in and out of her pussy like an animal—like a predator. She opened her eyes to the sight of his clenched jaw, his gritted teeth, his corded muscles, his bared incisors…

Zaab threw his head back on a deafening roar that bubbled up from his throat and reverberated throughout the jungle. He impaled her cunt over and over, never stopping his thrusting, as he pumped her cunt full of cum. She cried out at the sound, her eyes widening, the instinctive need to clasp her hands over her ears thwarted by the vines that held her pinioned to the cold ground of the jungle.

"Mine," he hissed into her ear as his climax began to wane. "My cunt."

He continued to stroke his massive erection in and out of her flesh, his cock still not satiated. But then neither was her body replete. The hallucinogen had made it so it would be hours, perhaps days, before her pussy felt satisfied.

The general fucked her for endless hours that night, stopping occasionally to feed and care for her. And he did take good care of her, Dee would later admit. He forced her to drink liquids even when she didn't feel thirsty, growled at her to eat the food bits he placed in her mouth even when she complained she wasn't hungry.

And always he fucked her. Violently. Endlessly. Gluttonously.

After several hours of mating, he finally cut the vines from her body, freeing her. But he didn't let her go, of course, didn't give her the chance to escape from him again. He twined his large, warm body around her smaller one instead, providing her with warmth as they drifted off into slumber.

Chapter 3

Zaab carried his naked slave on his back as they made their way through the highlander jungle. Harnessed to him by a leather-like contraption Dementians often used when carrying their young, he was taking no chances with either his captive's safety or with the chance that she might escape him for a third time.

Dee Ellison—he knew her birth name. It had been the first piece of information he had extracted from the slave Zidia when she had been captured by the Mantus Hoard and sold to the Myng Hoard.

Zidia had tried to escape Dementia with Dee, he knew, but of course, the lasses had failed. On a planet where no female births ever occurred it would be foolhardy to let even one wench of childbearing years leave it. Without the humanoid female slaves available to breed, there would be no such thing as Dementia, for their numbers would die out until their species was extinct—a fact Dementian males were careful to keep quiet about to outsiders.

His warlord friend Jek Q'an Ri had once told him that mayhap his species should try love on the wenches instead of slavery. But Zaab failed to see the difference between the wife of a warrior and the *zahbi* of a Dementian. Neither was given the choice concerning whether or not they could leave the male who had captured them. Neither was permitted to touch another male after mating.

Insofar as Zaab was concerned, Dee Ellison's fate had been sealed from their first meeting…and her first escape.

The first time the general had laid eyes on her she had been attempting to steal a spacecraft vessel from Stone City with the slave Zidia. His fighters had captured Zidia within minutes, but Dee Ellison had managed to escape into the lowlander jungle.

If he hadn't been immediately taken with the lass upon first glance, then by the time the wench had managed to thwart his attempts at capturing her, he had been consumed with her. Zaab had thought back on the lass often after that eve, wondering if she had met a bad end, wondering too if she'd been captured by another male.

Three months later Zaab had caught Dee stealing meat from the communal hut of the Mantus Hoard. His first reaction had been surprise at seeing her—alive and not yet enslaved to another. His second reaction had been admiration, for 'twould have taken more than a wee bit of cunning to survive alone and unaided within the jungle for so long. His third reaction had been a mix of lust and possessiveness—he wanted her and he wanted no other male to touch her. His fourth reaction had been anger, for the wench had managed—again—to escape him.

The admiration, lust, possessiveness, and anger coalesced into obsession. He was obsessed with Dee

Ellison, he knew. Mayhap he would always be obsessed with her.

"I'm thirsty," she whispered from the harness strapped to his back, the first words she had spoken in hours. "May I have a drink?" When he didn't answer right away, she amended her statement. "May I have a drink, Master?"

Her voice was scratchy, her throat parched. He hated that he cared so much, but there it was. Ammunition she could use against him if she knew of his obsession. He steeled his jaw and answered her. "We will stop at the next stream, slave."

Fifteen minutes later, Zaab's green eyes watched as his naked obsession drank from the pure waters of a highlander stream. She was on her hands and knees, her back to him, cupping water and lifting it to her face for refreshment. His gaze strayed to her cunt.

Puffy. Pink. Pretty.

His.

Dee gasped when Zaab's hands roughly grabbed her hips, then groaned when he slid his huge cock into her pussy from behind. "Beg me, slave," she heard him grit out. "Beg me."

On her hands and knees, impaled to the hilt, her sensitive breasts dangling, she had never been more aroused. Or more worried about her body's reaction to the general.

He slowly slid his cock out, then back in, teasing her with the promise of ecstasy. She shuddered, wanting more. "I beg you," she murmured.

"I didn't hear you, lass." He gave her two more long, deep strokes.

"I beg you!" she gasped. "Please fuck my pussy, Master."

He palmed her breasts from behind. "Whose pussy?" he growled.

"My—your—*your* pussy." She groaned when his fingers began plucking at her nipples. "Please fuck your pussy, Master!"

He took her hard, animalistically, plunging in and out of her flesh like the predator he was. His growls punctured the night, his masculine scent perfumed the air.

"Harder," Dee moaned, throwing her hips back at him. *"More."*

His growls grew louder, more reverberating, as he fucked her harder, the sound of their flesh meeting an aphrodisiac. "Do you like this, little lass?" he ground out. His fingers dug into the padding of her hips as he pummeled her cunt with deep, possessive strokes.

"I love it," she gasped. It was the truth. An unsettling truth. She would be no man's slave.

Dee came violently, her entire body shuddering on a groan loud enough to wake the dead. She could feel Zaab's cock ruthlessly plunging into her from behind, over and over, again and again. She could hear his low, possessive growl, could feel his powerful muscles tensing...

"Zahbi," he growled as she felt his hot cum pour into her. *"Mine."*

Panting for air, her eyes closed in a euphoria more hedonistic than the one brought on by the vines. She was on the verge of orgasming again when she cried out instead, shocked and in pain when two incisors sliced into her shoulder. "Zaab—don't kill me! No—please!"

"Mine," he growled against her shoulder as he lapped up the blood the pinpricks had made. *"All mine."*

Dee came harder than she'd ever come before, moaning and groaning while she met each of his animalistic thrusts with one of her own. The orgasm was endless, intense—all consuming. Blood rushed to her face, heating it. Blood rushed to her nipples, elongating them until they stabbed Zaab's palms.

"Oh god," she whimpered as they came down from the high together. "Oh god."

Chapter 4

One week later

Dee didn't know what to make of anything. She was Zaab's slave—one slave in a harem of thirty. And yet the only woman he touched, the only woman he even looked at, was her. The other females were but serving girls to him, whereas she was…well she didn't know what she was. She only knew that she hadn't been given much in the way of chores beyond feeding him, bathing him, and fucking him.

Confusing.

Equally confusing was the fact that she was growing to care for him. She didn't know how that had come to happen, or when precisely he had gotten under her skin, only that he had.

Zaab was rough and stern—but only to others. He was ferocious and deadly—but only to others. Where Dee was concerned, Zaab was different somehow. His speech was gentler when she was around. His conduct was more relaxed and personable with her than with anyone else. Almost as if…

She snorted at her thoughts. Dementian males did not *love*. Emotions like that were not in their genetic make-up.

Were they?

She sighed. Did it matter?

Naked, for slaves were always naked, Dee padded over to the window of the large thatch and stone hut that was Zaab's home and stared out of it, her thoughts a million miles away. She'd been in Dementia for over a year now and was a much different woman from the carefree one who'd once called Earth home.

Would Earth feel like home now, she wondered. Would she be able to forget this past year and fit in with other humans again if she found a way to return? Did she want to?

One thing was for certain, Dee thought on a sigh. It would be difficult, to say the least, to pretend that she was just like every other human. She would be forced to keep her silence about Dementia for fear of being institutionalized. She would be forced to do her damnedest to erase the past from her memories for fear that she'd slip up and start talking about life in the alien jungle.

And she would be forced to find pleasure with a human male. As if a human male could ever hope to compare…

"What troubles you, lass?" Zaab asked the question before leaning down to place a kiss on her shoulder.

Dee jumped, startled, for she hadn't heard him come in. "You frightened me," she breathed out, turning around to face him.

He snorted at that. "'Tis doubtful that ten charging *liats* could frighten you." He lowered his face to her chest, popped a nipple into his mouth, and began suckling.

She smiled, proud that he found her a force to be reckoned with. And then she moaned, turned on by the attention he was laving on her breasts.

Zaab raised his head a few minutes later, his green eyes clashing with her blue ones. He reached for her golden hair, his fingers running through it. "'Tis beautiful, lass. As are you."

More soft words. At this rate, she'd never want to leave him. "Thank you," she whispered.

They stood there in silence, gazing at each other, neither of them speaking a word. But finally, long moments later, Zaab broke the silence. "Come to my bed, *zahbi,*" he said softly, "I cannot sleep without you in it."

Don't do this, she thought. *Don't make me love you.*

But when he laced his fingers through hers and gently guided her to the bed, she knew deep inside that it was too late.

She had been lost to Earth from the moment their gazes first clashed in Stone City.

Chapter 5

The Feast of Beginnings
One week later…

General Zaab, the Alpha Male of the Mantus Hoard, the Supreme Master of the Highlanders, leaned back in his chair as he watched three naked slave girls dance for him. This eve was special for the feast they were partaking of was held in honor of Jaaker, the male ape-god who had breathed life into the first of their species.

Zaab cared not that the males of his hoard were touching and fondling the three slaves as they danced by. Slaves were expected to give their bodies not only to the master, but to his friends and family members as well. Or more to the point, they were expected to give their bodies freely for the use of any Dementian male, until she was claimed as a *zahbi* by the male who impregnated her.

In the eyes of Zaab, Dee was already his wife. Yet he knew the others would not see it thusly. Her belly was not ripe with child, therefore, 'twas impossible to make a public claim on her. He had marked her privately when he'd bitten into her shoulder that eve at the stream, yet insofar as he knew none of the Dementian males had seen her branding.

He knew they hadn't. He'd permitted no other males to be near her.

Zaab's green eyes darted up when he saw Dee walk into the communal hut carrying trenchers. His entire body stilled. Who had told Dee to come to the feast? Had he not given orders that—

"Such beautiful breasts you have, my dear," the leader of the Myng Hoard told Dee as he cupped them, pulling her to his side. "You have nipples like berries."

Dee blushed, clearly not knowing what to do or say.

"Bend over, wench," another gorilla fighter called out. "I want to see what your cunt looks like. Mayhap 'tis worthy of milking my cock."

Zaab exploded from his chair, leaping onto the table before them in one swift action. Growling, he backhanded the fighter who had thought to fuck her, blood spurting from the male's nose as he fell to the ground.

Dee turned wide blue eyes on him.

"What is this?" the leader of the Myng Hoard asked, offended. "You have insulted my fighter!"

"He has insulted me!" Zaab bellowed. "That wench he thought to fuck is my *zahbi*!"

Dee's mouth dropped open. It was then that Zaab realized she'd had no idea what *zahbi* meant…until this moment.

"Well I…I…did not know," the leader sputtered. "You have not publicly claimed her, General Zaab. She wears no belly chain." The leader of the Myng Hoard, clearly not wanting bad blood with the Mantus Hoard, nodded respectfully down to Dee.

"Congratulations on your pregnancy, lass. 'Tis honored you are to bear the heir of the Mantus."

Zaab glanced away, preparing to be publicly humiliated. The moment Dee told them the truth he would look the fool for caring so deeply for a wench he had not—

"Thank you," Dee said simply.

Zaab's body stilled.

"I'm sorry you were confused, but he was planning to publicly claim me at the feast tonight."

Zaab glanced up at her, warily meeting her gaze.

"Weren't you, Zaab?"

"Err..." He was shocked. He could scarcely believe Dee had defended him and his honor before the others. "Aye," he muttered.

"Well then," the leader of the Myng Hoard interrupted, his attempt to keep any potential brawls at bay obvious. "Let us get on with the claiming then."

* * * * *

A little embarrassed, but mostly aroused, Dee sat on Zaab's lap, her back to his chest, and eased her pussy down onto his cock until she enveloped him. She heard his grunt of pleasure when he was seated to the hilt, then moaned when his fingers began plucking at her nipples.

The gorilla fighters watched, her legs splayed wide before them, as she began to bounce up and down on Zaab's cock, moaning and groaning from the pleasure of it. She knew they could hear the suctioning sound her cunt made as it enveloped him, knew that they could smell the scent of her arousal as her tits jiggled up and down for their viewing pleasure.

But then that was the point. For Zaab to publicly bring her pleasure, for Zaab to publicly brand her as his own.

"Beg me," Zaab murmured in her ear. "Beg your Master for his cum, slave."

"Please," Dee gasped, bouncing up and down as hard and as fast as she could on his thick cock. "Please cum in your cunt, Master!"

She groaned when Zaab grabbed her roughly by the hips and, with a growl, began pumping his cock into her pussy like an animal. She closed her eyes, her head falling back on his chest, and bared her neck to him in front of one and all while he fucked her.

His hand reached around and he began stroking her clit while he lowered his face to her neck. She came the moment his incisors broke the skin there, moaning loudly as she rode out the climax.

This time he had marked her neck, not her shoulder. She wasn't precisely certain of the deeper meaning, but she was certain there was one.

The gorilla fighters applauded, shouting out bawdy remarks. "Fuck her harder!" one bellowed. "Spread the lass's cunt lips apart for us!" another shouted.

Zaab, arrogant as ever, did both. Dee closed her eyes and reveled in another orgasm, gluttonously loving every moment of it. She'd never been showcased like this before, had never been fucked in front of hundreds of men while they all sat around and watched her moan and groan with pleasure.

When it was over, when Zaab spurted his hot cum into her cunt on a roar, a belly chain was handed to her Master, which was then placed around her middle.

Dee glanced over her shoulder and smiled up at him. Their bodies were still joined together. "I guess this means I'm your wife now."

Zaab leaned down and kissed the tip of her nose. "Aye. Your Master will always cherish you, little lass."

Epilogue

Naked, Dee rubbed her belly, which was ripe with Zaab's heir. She laid down on the sweet, fragrant grass, then spread her legs wide open for her Master. She smiled when he lowered his face to her cunt and began to lazily lap at it. "Mmm. That feels so good, Zaab."

He purred low in his throat as he playfully nibbled on her clit. "Mmm. It tastes so good, *zahbi*."

She closed her eyes and smiled dreamily while he pleasured her outside under the warm rays of the red-tinted sky. Long minutes later, when they'd both had their fill, she made an announcement that would sound ludicrous coming from any woman but Dee. "We're going to have a girl."

Zaab's body stilled. He raised his face from between her legs. "'Tis sorry I am, Cherished One," he said quietly as he gently rubbed her belly. "But Dementians can only breed males."

"We're having a daughter," Dee said simply, nodding firmly.

Zaab snorted, a half grin on his face. "I suppose were it possible you would find the means to bear one."

She chuckled at that. "Yep." And then she reached out a hand. "Come up here and lie beside me where I can see you over my belly, you lovable oaf."

"Oaf," he growled, coming up to lie beside her. "Is that any way for a *zahbi* to talk to the Master who loves her?"

She smiled, snuggling into his warmth and resting her head on his muscled chest.

Together they fell asleep under the warmth of the red-tinted sky.

Dragon's Mistress

Written by

Joanna Wylde

Chapter 1

"You've got to be kidding," Dani said with a laugh to the man on the view screen.

He smiled blankly at her. "No, Miss," he replied in a neutral tone of voice.

He was a young man, in his early 20s at most, wearing the livery of the Von'hot household. The Von'hots ruled the system, but Dani wasn't intimidated by their power. She could tell he was uncomfortable with his assignment, but he tried to cover that unease with professionalism. "His Grace has specifically requested your services for the evening. We'll be sending a car for you shortly before sundown. Please be prompt, as His Grace appreciates timeliness in all his people."

"I'm not one of his people," Dani replied with a tight smile, trying to hide her annoyance at his attitude. "I'm a representative of the Pleasure Guild here on a diplomatic passport. And besides that, I'm retired. I no longer entertain clients."

The messenger's mouth gaped. Clearly, he had never heard anyone say "no" to his master before.

"But— "

"Please let Lord Von'hot know that I am flattered by his invitation, but that if he would like professional entertainment for the evening he should consider contacting *local* representatives of the Pleasure Guild. I've met the Guildmistress here in the capitol, and I've found her to be a competent and professional woman. I'm sure that she'll be able to find someone to take care of His Grace's needs. After all, it would be unpardonably rude of me to simply step in and take a contract in her city. Goodbye."

Dani reached over and turned off the screen with a decisive click, enjoying the look on the young man's face as she did so. She had no idea why Lord Von'hot had sent her such an invitation, and she didn't care. She was on vacation, and no man—even one who owned his own planet—was going to mess up *her* plans.

She stood and walked over to the balcony. Stepping out, she shook out her long, blond hair and gazed at the city before her. The view was stunning—her hotel room was on the 700th floor of the building, high enough that the atmosphere was thin and the air cold. Of course, none of that bothered her, as her balcony was enclosed in a force field that kept it comfortable. She leaned against the railing, somewhat amused by its presence. It was strange, but even after hundreds of years of technological development, humans still liked their balconies to have solid, visible railings no matter how unnecessary they were for safety reasons. After all, the shield would catch her if she fell.

Around her balcony, the spires of a thousand buildings reached up into the sky. More than a 100 million people lived there, according to the tour she'd taken the day before. It was a wonderful place for a vacation, even better for a vacation paid in full by the Guild. A small satisfied smile crept across her face at the thought. Serving as a diplomatic courier had its perks.

A chiming noise sounded softly through the air. Another call, she realized with a sigh. She walked back into her room toward the view screen terminal.

"Yes?" she answered politely as a face shimmered into focus.

"Dani, darling!" her caller trilled. The Guildmistress' perfect features smiled at her from the small screen.

"Hello, Guildmistress Karya," Dani said, her pleasure at this call genuine. "So good to hear from you again. I had a wonderful time at the reception last night. I can't tell you how long it's been since I've enjoyed a party that much."

Karya smiled back. She was a middle-aged woman, probably in her late 50s, yet she was still stunningly beautiful. Dani had heard stories of Karya's youthful conquests during her younger days. At the time they had seemed impossible to believe—she had been mistress to the old emperor himself, or so they said. But having met her, all the stories made sense. She was both beautiful and intelligent. No wonder the Guild's high council had been after her for years to take a leadership role. But she refused to move, saying she loved her home on Von'hotten too much to leave.

"Dani, my dear," Karya said. "You made quite an impression on our guests last night! I understand that Lord Von'hot's people have been in touch with you?"

"Oh, that," Dani sighed, making a disgusted face. "Don't worry, I got rid of them. I know better than to poach on your turf, Guildmistress Karya."

Karya looked startled, then burst into laughter.

"You'll never get far in the Guild hierarchy with a blunt attitude like that, child," she said, wiping tears of mirth from her eyes. "I've heard you were straight-forward, but my goodness!"

Dani laughed with her.

"Well, that may be, but I've never had much interest in administration anyway," she replied lightly. "Besides, I've decided to retire, as you well know. I'm just running a few errands and traveling right now. When I find someplace I like, I plan to settle down, perhaps buy a little house and live off my pension."

Karya raised one eyebrow questioningly.

"I have trouble seeing you settled in 'a little house' as you call it," she said with a smile. "You seem to like going where the action is. I heard you broke hearts all over Saurellian space before you returned to the Empire. Don't tell me you'd be content for more than a week in some boring backwater, because I simply won't believe it."

"Well, believe what you like," Dani said, still smiling. "I'm ready to relax and enjoy life. Too much work makes me a dull girl, you know."

"That's what I wanted to speak to you about, actually," Karya said, her smile fading. "I realize that you've stopped entertaining clients, something I completely understand because I've been retired myself for nearly 20 years. But our Lord Von'hot is apparently rather taken with you. It would be helpful to me if you would reconsider your decision to meet with him."

"Why is that?" Dani asked, startled. "It's totally against Guild protocol for me to meet with a client in your district, especially one like Lord Von'hot. Even if I wasn't retired, I know Guildmistresses who would have me thrown off planet for even considering it."

Karya chewed her lower lip gently, seemingly lost in thought for a second.

"May I come to your room, child?" she finally asked. "I'd feel more comfortable if we could discuss this in person. Do you mind?"

"Not at all," Dani said, truly confused. "Please, I would be happy to visit with you."

"Thank you," Karya said, smiling kindly. I'll be there in about half an hour."

Dani nodded, then switched off the terminal.

*****

Karya swept into Dani's suite of rooms in a haze of perfume. A small, timid looking woman followed her, carrying a large package.

"Calanna, wait in here," Karya said to her assistant, waving toward the couch. "Dani, can we speak on your balcony? We're far less likely to be overheard out there," she added giving Dani a confidential smile. They walked together out on to the balcony. Karya turned to her, her expression grave.

"It's difficult to explain all of this, Dani," she said with a sigh. "Normally I wouldn't share this information at all, but under the circumstances it seems necessary. You'll need to keep this to yourself, of course. It isn't exactly public knowledge within the Guild," she added with a meaningful stare. There was power in that look and Dani had to stop herself from squirming like a chastened youngster. No wonder so many movers and shakers in the Guild feared this woman, she thought. She'd met Imperial commanders with less authoritative gazes.

"For some reason, Lord Von'hot has been less than cooperative toward the Guild since he inherited the title last year. He allows us to continue our work here, but he hasn't been very forthcoming about policing the unauthorized pleasure houses and brothels that are always springing up in the city. He's also cut off several other sources of revenue, and we've recently discovered his people have been working against us on a number of business ventures. To be quite honest, it's undermined our position here considerably. We've been keeping the situation quiet, of course. The last thing we want is for every Lord and ruler throughout the Empire to follow suit."

Dani gasped. The implications for the Guild were too horrible to imagine—for centuries the Guild had maintained a monopoly on the pleasure industry, protecting their members and keeping them safe from exploitation. How many thousands, hundreds of thousands of women, would find themselves without protection if the Guild faltered? They had always been completely independent of local politics…

"How have you managed to keep this a secret?" she whispered, stricken. "I've never even heard rumors about this."

"We've been extremely cautious," Karya said, suddenly looking her age for the first time. "It's why I've been stationed here, to keep an eye on things. Lord Von'hot is a very dangerous man, and he has peculiar ideas on how his people should live. His entire family has always been that way. I'm sure you've noticed the lack of slaves here?"

"Yes," Dani said, thinking quickly. "It's actually one of the things I've liked best about this planet."

"Yes, we all like it," Karya said absently. "After all, the Guild has never allowed members to keep slaves. In fact, we've always felt a certain natural alliance with the Von'hots, a shared sense of values because of it. After all, they outlawed slavery five hundred years ago. I suppose it's part of what led us to lower our defenses here…"

Her voice trailed off, and she seemed lost in thought, almost sad. Dani coughed uncomfortably. She realized she was getting a glimpse of Karya that few people saw. The older woman blinked several times, then turned back to her.

"Drake Von'hot is very subtle, far more subtle than his older brother ever was," Karya continued. "In the time since he's inherited, Drake has eroded our power here to the point that we no longer have access to intelligence about his troop movements. We haven't been able to manipulate the financial markets for months, and he's even managed to have considerable assets confiscated or frozen. All of this has been done behind the safety of dummy corporations, of course. We can't prove anything.

"The worst, though, it our loss of control over the pleasure houses," she said, her face grim. "More than 200 Guild-owned pleasure houses have been shut down or gone out of business in the past year. Independent contractors have taken over. And you know what that means."

Dani nodded, her stomach twisting in knots at the thought. Independent pleasure workers, without the power of the Pleasure Guild behind them, were open to exploitation. Often all their money went to pimps, and they rarely had any future or retirement. Even the most foolish of Guild workers had a solid future following retirement. She had seen first-hand what could happen to women in that situation in the mining belts and space stations of the disputed territories. It wasn't pretty.

"What is he thinking?" she asked, genuinely confused. Usually rulers were welcoming to Guild workers. They paid their taxes and helped keep crime under control. Lord Von'hot's attitude simply didn't make any sense.

"I have no idea," Karya said, holding her hands out in a gesture of helplessness. "I've been to any number events with him since he came into power following his brother's death, and he's hardly acknowledged me. He's never been willing to meet with Guild representatives in a formal capacity at all. That's why I was so surprised to hear he had an interest in you. Have you even met him?"

"No," Dani replied, deeply confused. Aside from her fellow Guild members and the people at the diplomatic reception last night, she hadn't met anyone on Von'hotten.

"Well, it would be a great service to the Guild, and to me personally, if you would meet with him," Karya said with a sigh. "I realize you've retired, but this is the best chance we've had to get close to him since we realized what was happening. We can't afford to let it slip through our fingers."

"Yes, of course," Dani said, a feeling of helplessness coming over her. During her time with the Guild she'd entertained hundreds of clients, but always men of her own choosing. She didn't care for Lord Von'hot's attitude, simply ordering her to appear at a given time. But the Guild needed her; there was no escaping that fact. She owed her Guild sisters everything. She wouldn't fail them now.

"How shall I make the arrangements?" she asked, looking up at Karya with confusion. "I have no idea how to contact him," she added with an uneasy laugh. "I suspect he's not listed in the city directory…"

"I'll take care of that," Karya said, giving her a relieved smile. "You'll be well-compensated for your time and effort. Simply try to find out as much about him as possible. I don't have a specific assignment for you, just to get close to him. Anything you can tell us is helpful."

"I'll do my best," Dani said, looking at Karya earnestly. "I know my duty."

"Thank you, child," Karya said. "I knew I could count on you. Now, let's go back inside. I've brought you a special outfit to wear, and some jewelry. I thought you deserved something new and lovely, seeing as you're willing to do this favor for me."

"Thank you, Guildmistress," Dani said, startled.

"Call me Karya, child," the older woman said with a graceful smile. "The Guild is fortunate to have you among its members."

Chapter 2

She was stunning, Drake thought as he watched her step gracefully out of the air transport he'd sent to collect her. She was so beautiful it was unreal. Tall and slim, her white-blond hair cascading down her back like a curtain—just the sight of her was enough to make his breath catch.

When he'd first seen her at the reception last night, he hadn't thought she could possibly be as lovely in person as she'd been on the screen. Ostensibly, he'd been overseeing parts of his spymaster's surveillance of the reception last night because they suspected the Kelmorian ambassador would be meeting a key contact from the Imperial court that night, a contact Drake might recognize. Only Drake knew the real reason he'd been watching. He was looking for her; she was the key to his plans. The work of the past three years, all his plans and those laid by his brother, depended on her.

What he hadn't counted on was her affect on him. He'd wanted her, wanted her naked and spread under him. Wanted her in his bed, on his desk, against the walls of his palace. He wanted to fuck her long and hard, until she screamed in pleasure.

He wanted her so badly that he hadn't slept the night before. When it came time to summon her, he hadn't needed to feign his desire to his spymaster or guardsmen. It radiated from him, visible to all around him. In a way this was a stroke of good luck as it made the stories he intended to tell them all the more plausible. But it could complicate things as well.

He strode off his private balcony and across his bedroom. His guards snapped to attention as he walked past them and out the main doors of his suite. She was coming up the stairs, escorted by his assistant. His throat tightened and his cock stiffened as she came closer.

She was wearing a garment formed from filmy black scarves. With each step, they outlined her exquisite form, revealing and enveloping her charms all at once. He was filled with a burning desire to rip them off her body, exposing her for what she was. Her eyes met his, then, and he stopped breathing all together. A brilliant blue, they sparkled with the force of her personality. She was curious, intelligent. Powerful. He could see it all in a glance. He recognized her look. It was the same look he saw in his own eyes. With a quiver of anticipation, he realized that he had finally met the woman who might be his equal.

The thought sent a surge of lust so strong through his body that he almost gasped. He hardened as she approached, fighting the desire to cover his arousal like a teenage boy. What would it be like to touch her? He thought he might explode into flames at the mere thought…

"Lord Von'hot?" she said lightly, looking him up and down with a measuring glance. "I don't believe I've had the pleasure of meeting you before now."

"No," he said in a rasping voice, taking her outstretched hand and gently turning it over to kiss it. Her skin was smooth and supple under his lips, and he allowed his tongue to ever so lightly graze her palm. He felt a shiver go through her, and a surge of pure, masculine triumph welled within him. This woman might have the power to stun him with her presence, but he had power over her, too. "But I saw you at the reception last night, and was quite taken with your beauty."

"I wasn't aware you were at the reception last night?" she asked, her face registering polite surprise. He was willing to bet she was well aware he hadn't been present at the reception. He smiled at her smoothly.

"I was spying on the guests," he said, watching her reaction carefully. If she thought anything of his admission, she didn't betray it in her face. Good. She could dissemble, regardless of her feelings.

"How charming," she said, maintaining her polite smile.

"Thank you," he replied, drawing her hand into the crook of his arm. He started strolling slowly down the hall, guiding her. "My name is Drake, by the way. It could be rather awkward if you call me 'Lord Von'hot' all evening."

"I'm Daniella," she replied without looking at him. "Dare I ask where we're going?"

"Of course," he murmured, glancing over at the smooth perfection of her face. "I've arranged dinner and some private entertainment for us. I hope you'll enjoy it."

"I'm sure I will," she said, a chill in her voice. She didn't like his attitude, he realized. She probably thought he was rude. The thought amused him. "Thank you so much for inviting me," she added.

"The pleasure is all mine," he replied, drawing his breath in deeply. She smelled like flowers, light and fragrant. He wondered what she tasted like, and the thought nearly unmanned him.

Regardless of his long-term plans for her, she was his to enjoy for the night, he thought with satisfaction. He planned to use her well.

Chapter 3

She had never seen anything like Lord Von'hot's palace. It took every bit of Dani's willpower to keep her eyes focused directly ahead, rather than staring around with her mouth gaping. The walls were made of some crystalline rock that seemed to have been grown, rather than fashioned. There were guardsmen everywhere, dressed in dark uniforms and carrying frightening weapons of a kind she'd never seen before. The walls were hung with portraits, formally dressed men and women whose visages reeked of power and privilege.

How had she ended up here? She simply hadn't understood just how wealthy a man like Lord Von'hot must be when she'd originally turned down his invitation. He owned an entire star system and a confidant of the emperor, her mind whispered in panic.

And she was just a single pleasure worker, sent to spy on him.

She stole a glance up at him from beneath her lashes. He was tall, with hair so black it seemed almost bluish in the light. His skin was alabaster white, his cheekbones high and sculpted. His eyes were turned to the corridor ahead of them, but she couldn't forget the dark intensity of his black gaze.

He'd stared right through her, as if he could strip her naked with his vision alone. She'd felt helpless before him, a small and frightened animal caught in the glare of the predator's sight.

But with that fear was longing. His fingers were slender and strong; the touch of his lips against her hand had made her quiver with desire. She'd seen the bulge of his erection, something he hadn't bothered to try and hide from her. The thought of that thick, hard mass plunging into her body made her wet with longing. She'd never felt so instantly attracted to a man, and she had known hundreds of men in her time. She was in way over her head.

"This way," he said, guiding her through a magnificent doorway held open by two of his men. The room they entered was far smaller and more intimate than the broad hallway in which they'd met. In the center was a sunken stage, surrounded by a series of couches and low tables. An array of exquisite foods had been spread out, and she realized they would be dining in the Imperial style, lounging on the couches while they were entertained.

"Please, make yourself comfortable," he said, leaning down to speak directly in her ear with a soft voice. The hot wind of his breath made her shiver, tingles running down her spine. His hand touched her back, guiding her toward a low couch broad enough for several guests. She knew without asking that he would be joining her there.

She lowered herself, trying to appear polished rather than awkward. She rolled on to her stomach, leaning against the bolster that had been placed there for just such a purpose. He lowered himself next to her, bracing himself on one side, then reaching over to trail a finger down her cheek.

"Your skin is very soft," he murmured, his eyes mesmerizing her with their focused power. "May I kiss you?"

She nodded wordlessly, surprised he would ask. He leaned toward her, touching his lips to her with infinite slowness. His scent was all around her, she wanted to press herself forward into the kiss, but by then he had already withdrawn.

"When enjoying something as exquisite as this, it's best to move slowly," he whispered. Then he turned to face the stage, reaching out to ring a little bell.

Music filled the room, a strange type of composition she had never heard before. It was sibilant and rich, the instruments a strange mix that was new to her. A single flute wailed a plaintive melody, rising and falling against a background of other sounds.

"This is our own style of music," he murmured. "Von'hotten has always been a haven for artists and musicians, and I strive to support our unique heritage by commissioning works from local composers. This is something new. I hope you like it."

She nodded, captivated. She had no idea where the musicians were hiding, but they had to be close. Across the room, behind the screen? It was hard to tell. A woman dressed in a thin, filmy gown came and knelt before them, pouring some kind of drink into crystal goblets.

"Would you care for some wine?" Drake asked, lifting a glass to his lips. He took a sip, smiling in appreciation. "It's another local specialty. This vintage was grown and pressed on one of my own estates."

She nodded, and lifted her own glass. The flavor was rich and sensual, light but with a hint of spiciness that she couldn't quite place. She rolled it on her tongue with appreciation, then gasped as a tingle seemed to run from her mouth down her spine, pooling in the center of her being.

"It's also a light hallucinogen," he murmured, taking another sip. "Not enough to impair your judgment, of course. But we find its effects to be...stimulating."

The music rose around them, building in tempo and pitch. She looked down at the sunken stage with surprise to see several dancers moving in time. A woman and two men moved with lissome grace, wearing only the slightest of coverings draped around their hips. She took another sip of the wine, shivering from the sensation it sent down her spine. Drake reached over and held a small bite of fruit to her lips. She opened her mouth, gently sucking it in and reaching out with her tongue to lick his finger. He slid a little closer to her, leaning over to brush his lips against hers again.

The dancers were moving closer and closer together, their wisps of clothing falling to the floor. They moved with athletic grace, each step causing muscles in their arms and legs to tense and release in time with the music.

"They are well-known group," Drake whispered. She shivered as his breath danced across her earlobe. "Several of my nobles have had them perform on their estates. I thought you might appreciate seeing their art."

She nodded wordlessly, mesmerized by their gyrations. Though not Guild-trained, they truly were talented. The woman, a brunette with short curls bunched around her head and dark skin, had moved closer to the man in front of her. The other man faded into the background as the couple swayed together, their bodies brushing lightly. As Dani watched, the woman's brown nipples puckered in arousal, and she rubbed them sensuously against the man's chest. He responded by arching his back, proudly displaying a growing erection that jutted out toward his partner.

Drake's hand was rubbing the back of her neck, his movements following the same tempo as that of the dancers. She stretched, all but purring from the sensation. His touch seemed to reach deeply inside her, but she wanted more. She turned toward him, but his gaze was fixed on the dancers.

"Anticipation makes a meal more pleasurable," he said, his voice smooth as silk. "Watch the dancers."

She nodded, and turned her attention back to the show before them. The man and woman were kissing now, his light skin forming a stark and beautiful contrast with hers. A detached part of Dani's mind absently noted that the choreographer had taken exquisite care in selecting and pairing the dancers. Both were slim and athletic, but she was far smaller overall. She rubbed against her partner a moment longer, then started to slowly lower her body toward the ground, kissing him as she moved. The music started to slow, and a low-toned throbbing wound its way into the melody.

The woman was on her knees now, and her tongue darted out to kiss the tip of his cock. It twitched, and his head dropped back. She opened her mouth, slowly sucking the head of his erection into her mouth, then pulling back against it with deliberate motion. Her cheeks hollowed from the suction, she repeated the motion, reaching her hand around to cup his buttocks from behind. Bracing herself against his body, she started to bob her head back and forth on his hard length, deliberately, each thrust of her head punctuated by the music.

The other man slipped out of the shadows, coming to kneel behind her. He was much darker than either of the other two, his skin so dark he seemed like a shadow. Once again Dani gave a sigh of appreciation for the choreographer's skill. Seeing the three of them together was more than sexually stimulating. They were beautiful, each a slightly different shade of smooth skin, ranging from pale to darkest black. Exquisite.

The woman was still fully engaged in sucking her partner's cock as the second man reached his hands around her body to cup her breasts. His fingers grasped and pulled at her nipples, then one of his hands drifted to the cleft between her legs. He stroked her there for a while until her hips twisted and squirmed again his touch. He grasped her shoulders and pulled her away from the first man, his cock coming out of her mouth with one smooth motion.

The man gently pushed her down onto her hands and knees. Kneeling behind her, he slowly stuffed his own long, hard cock into her cunt even as the first man dropped to the floor before her. She leaned over and slowly sucked his erection back into her mouth, and the three squirmed against each other as they established a rhythm that had her impaled first on one end, then the other, over and over again.

Drake's hand against the back of Dani's neck had slipped lower, rubbing against the small of her back, and then her butt. As the threesome before them started writhing in the new position, he allowed his fingers to drop down between her legs, worming their way between the scarves that formed her outfit. She tensed as he moved, sensation spiraling through her body. She was already hot and wet for him, she had been since she'd first seen him, and the anticipation of his touch was killing her. She wanted his hand to find her center, to thrust against it and fill her. She wanted to be fucked, just like the dancer was being fucked. He was moving too slowly.

She squirmed against him, shifting her legs so they were further apart. He paused for a second, and then his fingers found their target. He grazed her clit, back and forth several times before pressing harder against it. Several fingers made their way into her hot slit, and she pushed her hips down against them, wanting more. She tried to turn to him again, but his casually draped arm held her in place. He wasn't ready for her to do any more than watch, she realized. Watch and feel, as his fingers explored her secrets.

The group before them was still moving in their graceful ménage, but once again they were shifting. The man on the ground reached up to grasp the woman, pulling her up his body. The man behind her sat back, and watched as his partner gently guided the woman's cunt down onto his waiting cock. The man on the floor leaned back on his elbows as she started riding him, his head thrown back in pleasure. Their efforts were starting to wear on them, and a thin sheen of sweat covered their bodies as they moved. Back and forth she went, his cock impaling her again and again.

Drake's hand was moving more quickly now, and Dani realized he was starting to breathe heavily beside her. She was glad to hear it—she hated the thought of him being unaffected by the performance while she was so aroused.

Abruptly, Drake pulled his hand away from her and sat up. She started to push herself up to join him, but he pressed a hand against her back and whispered, "Just watch. I'll take care of it."

She let herself fall back down, eyes fixed on the display before her. The second man had crept up behind the woman, placing his hands firmly against her back and pushing her down. She collapsed on the man below her readily, pressing kisses against his chest and neck. The man behind her was rubbing her back sensuously, massaging her tight little ass and rubbing his own cock thoughtfully.

Dani could feel Drake's hand on her own hips, lifting her and pushing up the scarves around her lower body. He slid one of the bolsters under her taut stomach, then slowly spread her legs wide. His fingers came down to rub her clit again, and she twisted as sensation pooled in her lower body. She felt open and swollen; she wanted him to fill her. His fingers slipped in and out, pressing within her cunt, but they weren't enough. Against her will, a small, mewling noise came out of her throat. Drake's mocking laughter danced across her spine, and he kept her held down before him with one hand pressed firmly against the small of her back.

On the stage before them, the woman had stopped kissing the man on the floor, holding herself straight and tense as the man behind slipped one finger back and forth across her back entrance. He pressed against her lightly, then placed the head of his erection against the tiny hole. She threw her head back in apparent strain as he started pushing into her slowly but surely, pinning her body against that of the man below her. Her face was clenched in a combination of pleasure and pain as his length sunk through her, until he hit bottom and all three were gasping. He reached one hand around her body, finding her clit and rubbing it hard. Then he pulled out and pushed back into her with a short, hard stroke. She gave out a little scream, and the man behind her moaned in answer.

Dani gasped as Drake's hand pulled away from her aching clit. Then she felt the round, smooth head of his cock pressed against her cunt and she shivered with anticipation. He moved into her steadily, the broad width of his erection stretching her moist opening as he pressed down. Wider and wider, deeper and deeper he moved, and she realized that she had seriously underestimated his size during her earlier appraisal. She'd assumed, from the bulge she'd seen earlier, that he'd been fully erect, but now she realized that he had still been at least partially soft. The monster that was entering her now was completely solid, a pillar of granite that would stretch her until she screamed from the pleasure of it.

A wave of hot lust hit her, smoothing the way for his penetration. She moaned, pressing back against him until he hit bottom, fully embedded within her flesh. She quivered in anticipation, knowing climax would be incredible when it finally arrived. He slipped back, then pushed forward again, this time hitting home with greater force. The motion pushed her forward on the couch and she gasped.

"Goddess," she whispered. "That's fantastic."

He gave a low, throaty laugh and moved faster. She could hardly pay attention to the dancers in front of her now. She was vaguely aware that they were writhing together with more urgency, but every bit of her ability to feel was taken up with the sensations that filled her with each of his thrusts. Then his hand stole back down around her body, rubbing and pressing her clit in time to his thrusts.

The pressure inside her was too intense to ignore, and she closed her eyes, reveling in the feel of him in and on her body. His fingers moved in time with his cock, and the coils of tension within her built to the point where she felt like screaming. Instead, she let her head drop down against the bolster and bit into it, completely taken over by raw need.

Then her orgasm hit, and her entire body stiffened and spasmed around his cock. He stopped moving, his body still hard with need.

"I love the way you feel right now," he gasped, lowering himself until he was draped across her back. He spoke directly into her ear, his voice urgent and compelling. "Every tremor, every breath is squeezing me. I'll come soon if we don't take a break."

She didn't reply. Instead, she simply turned her head against her shoulder and captured his lips in a deep kiss. Their tongues touched, flirting with each other, and she felt his massive length twitch within her. They were fully joined, two parts of the same being at that moment. She had never felt anything as exquisitely painful and pleasurable as this before.

He pulled his mouth away from hers, resting his chin on her shoulder. He should have been heavier, but he was balancing the bulk of his weight on his arms, careful of her comfort.

"We're missing the rest of their performance," he whispered. Dani giggled, having forgotten the dancers who were working so hard to entertain them.

She turned her attention back to the stage below them. The woman's head was thrown back and sweat ran down her body. Every part of her body was tense, and her face twisted in pleasure. She convulsed between the men again and again. The man behind her thrust harder, each motion bringing her down on her other partner with a force that rocked all three of them.

Dani could feel herself growing hot and wet again, and when Drake started moving his hard length slowly back and forth within her moist opening, she sighed in satisfaction. He thrust steadily, each motion causing delicious friction against her skin. The twists of desire sprang into life, sending tingles of pleasure through her. She could tell that it was getting harder and harder for Drake to control himself. His breathing grew harsh as he moved, then he was on his knees again, bracing himself against her shoulders as he pushed into her hard enough to rock the couch that cushioned them.

The entertainers were coming close to their own end. The woman had come one more time, her gasps ringing through the room. As her body tensed, the man behind her threw his head back and shouted as he came, his butt pumping into her spasmodically. This was too much for the man beneath them, who came with a moan. All three collapsed into a gasping pile of silky arms and legs, a tangle of satiated and exhausted flesh.

Watching them achieve their orgasm seemed to spur Drake on, and he moved more quickly. Again the sensations were climbing up through her body, dancing along her spine until she stiffened and twitched from the intensity of her feelings. The orgasm washed over her like a tidal wave, slamming her against the cushions with a force she'd never dreamed was possible. Drake gave a low, harsh groan, and then he was coming too. She could feel his hot seed pouring into her, filling her with his essence and pummeling her internally. He fell down onto her, crushing her down into the cushions, and struggled for breath.

She lay there, completely unaware of her surroundings for several moments. Then she felt him rolling off to the side. He turned her toward him, pulling her up onto his chest as easily as he might move a lifeless doll.

His pale skin was flushed, but his eyes were cool and dark. Assessing, even. He looked at her without expression, and a chill came over her. He seemed to be unaffected by what had just happened between them, as if this was no more than any other tumble between the sheets. She was dazed by the experience, the power of her climaxes. Sex had been her business since she'd become a woman. How was it that things would be so different with this man?

"Kiss me," he whispered.

She dropped her lips to his with unfeigned enthusiasm. His lips were soft against hers, and where before he'd been the ravisher, the seducer, this time it was her turn. She nipped at them, allowing her tongue to dart out and slip between his lips, then playfully retreat. She kissed him along his jaw line, down his neck and against his powerful chest.

What had happened to his clothing? she wondered. He was naked now, yet she couldn't remember him taking the time to undress. She was still wearing her gown, although it had been pushed to her waist. She was naked beneath. His clothing was unimportant, though. All she cared about was touching him.

She kissed along his chest, visiting each nipple and laving them with her tongue until they stood in stiff peaks. One of his arms was draped casually over his head, and his eyes were closed. His breathing was slow and regular now, and his look had softened into one of contentment.

She felt a stirring against her hip, and realized he was becoming aroused again. She dropped her kisses lower, drifting across his stomach towards his manhood below, just starting to awaken again. He stopped her, pulling her back up his body for another long kiss.

"Let's go to my chamber," he said, pulling her to her feet. He seemed to be completely comfortable with his nudity, something she appreciated. She liked a man who was self-confident and unashamed of his sexuality. The musicians and dancers had disappeared, leaving them alone in the dining room.

"I'm afraid I didn't take the time to enjoy the meal," she said, smiling at him and feeling almost shy. The sensation caught her off guard. When was the last time she'd felt shy? Yet with this man it felt as if she were embarking on something new and wonderful. It was hardly the usual client encounter.

"Are you hungry?" he asked, gesturing toward the table. "We can stay and finish if you like."

"I'd rather go with you now," she replied, allowing some of the longing he inspired in her to touch her face.

He nodded, then took her hand and pulled her across the room. A door opened before them. More guards, clad in black, carefully avoided watching them as they strode down the hallway. Another set of doors opened before them, and they entered a room that was large and formal. He pulled her across to another set of doors, leading her through a series of rooms that became smaller and more informal the further they retreated.

Finally, they entered what had to be his chamber, a large, airy space decorated in simple yet lush furnishing. Against one wall was a bed. One entire side of the room was taken up in windows overlooking the city. She hadn't realized how much time had passed, but it was full night out, and the buildings spread out before them sparkled like thousands of gems.

"These are my people," he said simply, gesturing toward the city with a sweep of his arm. "My family has ruled this system for a thousand years. Our family has been in power longer than the current imperial dynasty."

What could she say to that? Dani wondered. She was a courtesan, trained to deal with men of power.

But somehow, spouting out one of the light-hearted remarks she usually affected, seemed so inappropriate to the moment. They were alone in his room, she realized, the most private place in his palace. Yet not a single personal item seemed to be kept here. It was lovely, but completely devoid of personality.

There were no other people around, either. No guards and no sign of a spouse or children. She hadn't heard of any other family members, she realized with a start. Usually ruling families were surrounded by courtiers, hangers-on and distant relatives. This palace seemed all but empty.

"Where is your family?" she asked before she had time to think better of the question.

"I don't have any family," he said, looking at her with amusement. "Didn't Guildmistress Karya give you any background on me before sending you to spy on me?"

Her breath caught.

"You were monitoring our conversation?" she asked tightly, fear filling her. What would he do to a woman he'd caught spying?

"Of course," he said, his tone mocking. "I have to be very careful, you know. I find myself in a delicate position dynastically. My brother is dead, killed in the war against the Saurellians. I was his only heir, and now I'm alone. He served on the front, at the Emperor's personal request." He paused for a moment, allowing his words to sink in.

"If I were killed now, this entire system would be forfeit to the Emperor," he added.

She had no idea what to say in response to this revelation. Surely Karya had known that, but they hadn't had time to discuss the situation in depth. After all, she was a courier and courtesan, not a spy. Her only experience was bringing pleasure to others she thought frantically.

"I see," she said, stalling for time. He turned away from her again, and her eyes flew around the chamber, looking for an escape route, or something to use as a weapon.

"I doubt very much that you do see," he said, his face dimly lit by the lights of the city. There was bleakness in his voice that made her heart twinge. He looked so alone, standing there above his home.

"These people are utterly dependent on me," he said quietly. "There are more than 40 billion of them living in my territory, between the various planets, moons and stations. It's not a large system, but we've always enjoyed a high quality of life. There's no slavery here. My people are happy and healthy—hardly any choose to emigrate to other worlds. We were even spared the worst of the war. My brother and his men paid a high price to keep our young men out of the hands of Imperial recruiters."

She nodded, starting to understand.

"You're afraid that if something happens to you, your people will suffer," she said softly.

"Afraid?" he asked, laughing with a harsh, barking sound. "Afraid doesn't begin to express how

I feel about the Emperor taking control of this system. If I die, it passes into his hands directly. Then he can start slowly milking my people of everything we've worked so hard to accomplish. Of course, if he decides I've committed treason, things will get far worse. He has the option of liquidating the entire population, you know."

"No," she whispered a wave of nausea washing over her. "He wouldn't do that."

"Oh really?" Drake turned back to her, and for the first time that night she could see some real emotion in his face. "You don't know what he's capable of doing. I am. I was raised with him, attended school with him in the Imperial Capitol, Tyre. He counts me as a friend, at least for now. That's why I'm still alive. But he won't tolerate my refusal to cooperate with him much longer. I've refused to go along with his plans; I'm the only one of his nobles with the courage to stand up to him. He'll kill me just as easily as he had my brother killed."

"What plans?" she asked, afraid of the answer.

"Well, he feels that the Saurellians have gotten too much power. He wants to start fighting them again, to end the truce," he said. "That would be a disaster for our people. We don't have the strength, or the right, to continue fighting. Do you know how the war started?"

"I'd heard the Saurellians attacked several systems in the disputed region," she replied. "That they were seeking new territory."

"No, that's just imperial propaganda," he replied quietly. "I think you know better than to believe that. Didn't you hear another story while you were in Saurellian space?"

"Yes," she said quietly, looking out over the city. "I'd heard that the Emperor had liquidated an entire planet because their assembly refused to pay a new tax, and that the systems in the disputed regions asked the Saurellians to protect them. I didn't believe it, though, at least not the whole story. The Saurellians are very aggressive, and I had trouble believing the Emperor would kill billions of people over taxes."

"The Saurellians are aggressive, but they aren't greedy," he said quietly. "They started fighting the Empire because those people came to them, pleading for their lives. They knew they'd be next if the Emperor had his way. He'll do it to Von'hotten, too, if he feels we're defying him. I have to stop that from happening."

"And how do you plan to do that?" she asked, turning to look at him directly. There was a sorrow there, and deep compassion in his face. Compassion for her, she realized. A new wave of horror and nausea swept over her, and she fell to her knees. She suddenly realized that the only way he could afford to tell her this much was if he planned to kill her.

"Oh, no, I don't want to know," she whispered. He came and knelt before her, tilting her chin up with on finger. He leaned forward and gently kissed her, then sat back on his heels.

"It's too late, Dani," he said quietly. "I think you already know that."

"Why did you tell me?" she asked. To her surprise, the horror was passing. In its place was a new emotion, anger that he would drag her into this. Her voice grew stronger. "Is it because I dared to come here and spy on you? Are you out to destroy the Guild, in addition to committing treason against the Emperor? We're not part of your Empire, we don't want anything to do with this. Take care of your own problems."

"Oh, it's a Guild problem, too," he said.

"How do you figure that?" she asked, her voice cold with disgust. "We're neutral. We don't need your crap."

"No, you *were* neutral," he replied. "Until 25,000 licensed Pleasure Guild workers were killed when the Emperor liquidated the planet of Kelvani. The action took place without warning, and they weren't given the option of using their diplomatic immunity to escape."

She gasped, shaking her head in disbelief.

"I didn't hear anything about that," she said. "If that was true, I would have known. The Guild takes care of their own. Our Council wouldn't just let the Emperor get away with killing our people."

"They don't intend to," he said, his expression growing fierce. "Don't you realize that even the Guild isn't strong enough to confront the Emperor directly? Neither are the nobles of the Empire. Do you think we like seeing him do things like this? Our civilization has flourished for a thousand years, and now one crazed idiot is going to bring it crashing down around us. The Saurellians aren't going to stop him. They don't want to break the truce. It's up to us."

"Who is 'us'?" she asked suspiciously.

"The nobles and the Guild," he said. "Why do you think you're here?"

"I thought I was here to pleasure you," she said quietly. He gave her a mocking look. "Well, to spy on you then."

"Karya sent you because she believes we can trust you," he said quietly. "You're uniquely qualified to help us. You've been in Saurellian space, and you have contacts there. We know you've already helped at least one Imperial slave escape. Don't bother to deny it," he said, holding up one hand when she started to protest. "Dani, you've been very careful, but we know you're smart and you're loyal to the Guild. You're also the perfect go-between for the Saurellians and us because no one will suspect you. You aren't a Guild functionary, you hold no office and you have no power. In short, you're not important enough for the Emperor to suspect you."

Dani snorted at his description.

"No, don't be offended," he continued. "That's what makes you perfect for this role. Karya has had her eye on you for a long time. She trusts you, and I trust her."

"That's not what she says," Dani said, her anger growing. Who the hell did he think he was?

"Well, that's what she says when she's being spied on by the Imperial intelligence service," Drake said. He reached forward, clutching her shoulders in his hands and pulling her toward him. He stared into her face, as if he could make her believe him by sheer force of will. "This whole evening is a set-up. Karya and I have been building toward this moment for a year. We've carefully created a rift between me and Guild so that no one would suspect us of collaborating."

"What is the point of all this plotting?" she asked harshly. "What are you going to do, overthrow the Emperor?" she asked, laughing at the idea. As if anyone could topple a sitting emperor. The thought was ridiculous.

"I can't tell you that," he said, dropping his hands from her shoulder and sitting back. "I'll only tell you what you need to know. It's safer for everyone that way."

"Oh, Goddess," she whispered, searching his face as the realization hit her. They were planning to do that very thing. "You'll have to kill him."

"Yes."

"Oh, Goddess," she whispered again, and sat back heavily on the floor. Life had suddenly gotten far more complex than she could ever have dreamed. "I'm supposed to be on vacation, you know."

"Yes, I know," he replied. "I'm sorry, Dani, but it's already too late for you. You're part of this whether you like it or not. You're the only one who can help us."

"Why me?" she asked quietly. "Why did you have to pick me? There are thousands of other pleasure workers who've been in Saurellian space. Why couldn't you pick of them for this? I don't want this!"

"Because to carry out our plans, we'll need to work with the Saurellians," he said. "And you're the only pleasure worker with the connections we need. That slave you helped escape, her name was Calla? She's more than an escaped slave. She's become the daughter-in-law of the Saurellian Federation Council's President. She's going to be in Tyre over the next six months with her husband on a diplomatic mission, and you're the one woman in Imperial space she'll trust."

Chapter 4

He stared earnestly into her face, willing her to believe him. They were almost out of time. He'd managed to arrange a temporary power failure that would keep the Emperor's spies from listening in on them, but they would suspect something if the power didn't come back on soon.

She bit her lip, staring up at him with those stunning, unreal blue eyes. Despite the seriousness of their situation, he felt a twinge of desire for her. It filled him with dark amusement. Here he was, plotting to overthrow an emperor, and still all he could think about was bedding this incredible woman.

He was so caught up in his thoughts that it never occurred to him she would hit him.

The blow took him in the jaw, and he hit the ground with a thump. He gasped for breath as it had knocked the wind out of him. She stood over him, hands braced on her hips and glaring in anger.

"I may be a pleasure worker, but I will not let myself be used," she said with bitter venom. "I have no reason to believe you. You may kill me for this, but I'd rather be dead than betray my friends and my Guild. I have no reason to believe a thing you say."

"I can prove it to you," he said, fingering his jaw.

"How?"

He stood, watching her carefully. He wouldn't make the same mistake again, he thought.

"Take off your earrings."

"What?"

"Take off your earrings," he repeated. "Karya gave them to you earlier today, didn't she? For tonight."

She nodded, reaching up to take out the delicate silver baubles.

He reached out to take them from her. She handed them to him, and he turned them over in his hands. They appeared to be a random twist of silver wires and pearls, but he knew there was a pattern. There it was...he found the right spot and allowed them to interlock with each other. Then he held them up for Daniella to see. They had formed the delicate outline of a dragon, the mythological beast which was part of the Von'hot family crest.

"Where did Karya say she got these?" he asked quietly, handing them back to her.

"From her son," Dani whispered, looking up into his face.

"I gave her the earrings," he said quietly. She opened her mouth, but he cut her off. "I'm not going to tell you the whole story. There's no need for you to know any more, and too many people could suffer if anyone found out. But Karya is my mother, and we have been working together for years. Before he was killed, she planned all of this with my brother. Come over here."

He strode across the room to a small table. He picked up a small, hand-held illuminator, one with varying light frequencies. It was something that could be found in almost every home in the Empire. He turned to her.

"This is only visible with a specific frequency of light," he said quietly, punching a six-digit number into the wand. "It was tattooed into my upper arm as a child, to help them identify me if I was ever kidnapped."

He switched on the light, holding it up to his arm. Within the purplish light, the glowing outline of a dragon came into view beneath his skin.

"Hold up the earrings next to it," he said. She did, gasping. He watched her face, but he already knew what she was seeing. The delicate tracery of the wires and beads, held at exactly the right angle, matched his tattoo exactly. There could be no mistaking it.

"Do you believe me now?" he asked.

"You could have had those given to Karya," she said, shaking her head.

"Yes, I could have," he replied. "But how would have I arranged for her to give them to you? You know I'm telling the truth."

She was silent, a single tear welling up.

"I wish you weren't," she said. "How could all those people be dead, and none of us know about it?"

"He's not sane," Drake replied, filled with compassion for her. He remembered when he'd first heard the news, and realized that he no longer had a choice in fighting the Emperor. "Will you help us?"

"Yes," she whispered, reaching one hand up to wipe away the tears. "Yes, I will," she added, her voice stronger. He detected a note of steel in her tone, and he sighed with relief. Karya hadn't underestimated her.

"It's going to be very difficult for you," he said. "You're going to become my mistress. The Guild is going to expel you for turning against them, and you'll be publicly humiliated."

"I understand," she said, nodding her head with quiet dignity.

"When we go to Tyre, you'll be an outcast among the Guild members. And you'll be an outsider among the nobles. They won't look upon you as an equal, you know."

"I can handle that."

"There's one more thing," he said, "and this may be the hardest part of all. Within a day or two I can guarantee that the Emperor's people will contact you, try to recruit you to spy on me. You'll have to agree with them, and you'll have to keep up a convincing front that you're working against me."

"How will you know I'm not working against you?" she asked, looking at him coolly. All traces of tears were gone now.

"Because 25,000 of your Guild sisters will be counting on you to bring some kind of meaning to their deaths," he said. "Even if you betrayed me, I know you wouldn't betray them. Do we have a deal?"

"Yes," she replied. "We have a deal."

"Good," he said. He pressed a small button against the wall, and spoke with a commanding voice, "Please send us a tray of fruits, cheeses and wines."

"Yes, Your Grace," a disembodied voice replied. Drake turned back to her.

"In order for us to speak privately, I had to arrange for a 'random' power failure that cut off Imperial surveillance of this room. Ordering the food was the signal to restore the power, so they won't get suspicious and realize I know about their bugs. We have about three minutes until the power disruption ends," he added. "I'd like for them to think we've been doing things other than talking this entire time."

He gestured toward the bed, and she nodded, walking toward it quickly while shrugging out of her gown. She jumped up the three steps surrounding the high, canopied platform seemingly without a thought for her nudity, but Drake was struck silent by the sight of her. She was exquisite, perfect. Her soft, round butt swayed as she walked away from him. Her long, blonde hair hung to her waist in perfect ringlets. How did she do that, keep it so perfect even after all they'd done earlier?

"Drake, are you coming?" she asked, looking back to him with concern on her face. "We don't have much time."

He couldn't help it, he burst out laughing. The most beautiful woman he'd ever met was on his bed, demanding that he join her, and there wasn't even a hint of sexuality in her movements. It was just too funny.

She stared at him, confused. "What?" she asked.

"Nothing," he replied, shaking his head. "It's not important."

He walked slowly toward her. She had turned around on the bed, and he could just see her pink nipples peeking out through the curtain of her hair. He could feel himself hardening as he moved closer, his erect cock swaying and his balls tightening up in anticipation.

She was smiling now, leaning back on her elbows and her legs spread out wide before her. Her cunt was open and waiting for him.

"Come here," she whispered. "You know, before I never even got the chance to touch you, Drake, but if you're going to be taking me on as your mistress than I think you should probably get a taste of what I bring to the table. I may be retired, but I was very good at my job."

He climbed up onto the bed, looming over her. She reached down with one hand and firmly grabbed his erection, holding it just a little too tightly for comfort.

"I'm in this now," she whispered, her face all innocence. "But don't forget that you're in it with me. Screw me or my Guild over and I'll take you with me." She twisted him ever so lightly, for emphasis.

He froze, startled.

"I won't," he whispered, his mouth coming down over hers in a gentle kiss. She kept her hold on him, but loosened her fingers, sliding them up and down his hard length. He shuddered, sensation running from his center up his spine. She pulled her mouth away from his, and looked up at him.

"We're out of time," he said. "We've got to make this look good."

"That won't be a hardship," she replied softly. "Now, get on your back. I plan to charge you a great deal of money to be your mistress. I'd better start earning it."

He rolled onto his back, watching her as she moved to straddle him. She slowly lowered herself until he could feel her hot, moist cunt brush against him. His hips pushed up against her, trying to get in, but she pulled away.

"Oh, no," she said. "That's far too easy, Drake. Like I said, I want to earn my money."

She leaned over him, rubbing her breasts against his chest sensuously. Her nipples were tight, hard pebbles against him, and he groaned in pleasure. Then she kissed him, her lips light and moist against his. She teased him, nipping and lapping at him, then dropping little kisses along his jaw and neck. Her mouth worked its way lower, trailing fire along his chest. Lower and lower she moved, and then one hand was gripping the length of his cock. Her lips were almost there, and she felt his stomach muscles clench in anticipation.

She looked up at him through her veil of hair, her eyes filled with a look of power that said he might be ruler of the world, but for that moment she was his ruler. He closed his eyes and let his head fall back, content to be under her control for now.

Her tongue slipped out, tracing the little ridge that ringed the head of his cock. He shivered, quivering at her touch. She grasped him firmly in her hand, then pulled down on his skin. He felt sensitive, exposed. Then her tongue touched him again, this time right above her hand. She trailed it up along the underside of his erection and wiggled it against him as she reached the little notch below the head. His hips thrust up at her once, involuntarily. She laughed throatily, then her mouth engulfed him fully, sucking him into its warms depths.

She slipped down on him, sucking him in hard and then pulling back, her lips trailing over him. Her head moved down again, hot against him. She moaned, unable to control herself. Up and down she went, moving faster and faster.

The sensations built in him. He was so sensitive that the motions of her lips and tongue against him were almost painful. He was getting closer, his breath came faster and his heart pounded in his chest.

Her mouth pulled away from him, and she was sitting up, giving him that smile again. Then she was scooting up his body, her hair sending shivers through him as it trailed along his skin. She raised her hips and slid down over him; he grunted in reaction to her movement. She was a hot, tight glove enclosing him, squeezing him. Her hands were braced against his chest as she twisted her body against his, massaging him with her interior muscles. Then she froze, and he heard an embarrassed cough. She sat up, still impaled on his length.

Drake leaned up on his elbows and looked to see who had entered.

His spymaster was standing there, wearing the uniform of a servant and holding a heavily laden tray. The man looked up and down her body with interest.

"You requested food, Your Grace," the man said in dulcet tones. "Shall I put the tray on the table?"

"Yes," Drake said, his voice harsh. The witch had started squeezing him again as she sat their, her movements completely invisible to their audience. "On the table, that will be all," he gasped out.

The man gave him a sardonic look, then turned to set down the tray. He gave them a curt bow, then turned to leave the room. Drake let himself fall back down on the bed, straining as she continued working him deep inside. The door closed with a click, and she gave a tinkling laugh.

"What's the matter, Drake?" she asked, grinning down at him.

"I'll show you," he grunted, trying not to grin back at her. Moving quickly, he rolled her under him, thrusting deeply into her. She moaned, twisting against him as she brought her legs up and around to powerfully clasp his hips. Her hands reached down to his butt, digging into each cheek as she pulled him down into her. He drove down into her again and again, pushing as deeply as he could. He wanted to bury himself in her, to push so deeply into her body that the feel of him was imbedded in her. He realized he was trying to brand her, that he felt possessive of her.

She was whimpering now, and she bucked against him as he pressed her harder down into the bed. Her fingers dug deeply into him, raking up his back, leaving a trail of fire in his skin. She was marking him, he realized. The pain of her touch only made him more excited, more eager to possess her. She was wild, and she was his. But she wouldn't give in easily.

She whimpered again, and he could feel her starting to convulse around him. He gritted his teeth with exertion; he was so close. He slammed his cock into her again, hitting deep and hard and she exploded under him. She screamed a high-pitched wailing noise that cut through him. She squeezed him so tightly it hurt, her muscles seeming to scrape against his hypersensitive skin. His balls were hard, tight with his seed. He thrust one more time and then came, the hot liquid shooting out of him with explosive force. His blood roared in his ears, and he collapsed on her, gasping for breath.

After a moment to recover, he rolled off of her. She was still gasping and whimpering from her own release, but she rolled onto his chest and kissed him deeply.

"Will you mind being my mistress?" he asked her when they paused for air. She smiled down at him, her face flushed pleasantly pink from her exertions.

"Oh, no, I won't mind at all," she whispered. "I'm looking forward to it."

Chapter 5

"Guildmistress Karya?" Calanna's voice drifted softly into the room. Her voice was unsteady, off balance.

"Yes, child?" Karya asked, leaning back in her comfortable chair.

"You have a call, from Lord Von'hot," she replied, seemingly dazed. "Lord Von'hot, himself, not his secretary or anything..."

"I'll take it from here, Calanna," Karya said, careful to inject her tone with confusion. She had no doubt their conversation was being monitored by Imperial spies. Leaning over, she carefully switched on her screen. The picture she saw next was one of decadent debauchery.

Drake Von'hot was calling her from his bedroom. He was lounging back against a pile of silken pillows. Dani was kneeling before him, her blond hair draped across his lower body. Karya assumed she was performing fellatio, although it was hard to tell. With clinical detachment, she noticed the girl was the consummate professional. Nothing in her stance betrayed the fact that this most intimate of acts was being performed before a view screen.

"Guildmistress Karya," Drake said, his voice filled with smug triumph. "I thought I'd call and let you know myself that I've convinced Daniella here to come work for me, now." He reached down with one hand, patting her head as if she were some exotic pet.

"I see," Karya replied coldly. "You do realize that it is against our code for her to make a contract with you without Guild sanction. It is traditional for a man of your position to make such arrangements through the local Guild authority. In this case, that would be me."

"I don't think that's necessary," he replied, smiling at her. "As I'm sure you've noticed, the Guild no longer holds the same position in this sector that it once held. Daniella has already made her decision."

Karya's hands clenched against the armrests of her chair. Her voice betrayed no tension, however, as she calmly asked, "Dani, is this true?"

Dani lifted her head from Drakes lap, and turned to look into the view screen. Her face was flushed, her lips red and swollen. She had the look of a woman who had been well loved.

"Yes, Karya," she said, her voice filled with malicious glee. "Lord Von'hot's made me a wonderful offer too good to refuse. Especially since he'll be paying me directly, not through the Guild. I'm tired of giving my earnings away to people like you."

"Daniella, you do realize that if you do this, you'll be expelled from the Guild. We're here to protect you-" Karya said, but her voice was cut off by a scream in the outer office. Calanna burst through the door, crying. Behind here were six heavily armed men in Drake's livery.

"I've sent you an escort, Guildmistress," Drake said in a light, amused voice. Karya's gaze snapped back to the view screen. He was pushing Dani's head back down toward his hips, and smiling with satisfaction. "I've decided that we no longer need Guild administrators on Von'hotten. Of course, individual pleasure workers will be more than welcome to stay, if they so choose. You, however, are no longer welcome."

With that, the transmission ended. Calanna was kneeling at her feet, crying and begging the men not to hurt them. Karya looked at her captors with cool dignity, then took a deep breath and stood up.

"I assume you'll allow me to collect my things?" she asked quiet dignity. The troopers looked at each other, and then one stepped forward. With interest, she noticed his discomfort. He didn't approve of his orders, she realized.

"I'm sorry, ma'am," he said in a low voice. "But we've been instructed to escort you directly to the space port. Your ship is waiting."

"I see," she replied quietly. "Calanna, pull yourself together. They aren't going to hurt us."

Calanna, still whimpering in fright, slowly stood up. Karya grasped the younger woman's hand firmly, and together they followed the soldiers out of the room, out of the building, and into a waiting transport. Karya held herself with stiff dignity the entire time, looking neither right nor left.

In fact, she didn't allow herself to relax at all until several hours later, long after she'd left Von'hotten.

They allowed her to leave on a Guild ship, and in the privacy of her own cabin, Karya went into the fresher and turned on the faucet. The cool water ran out, and she splashed a little up on her face. Then she burst out laughing, grinning at herself in the mirror like a naughty child.

They'd pulled it off. Her boy had convinced Dani to work with him. He was every bit as smart as his father had been, she thought wistfully. If only his father was still alive…

She caught herself, her iron discipline shutting the thought out. He was dead and gone, no point in thinking of him. Now it was time to help her son and her Guild.

She walked out into her room, sat down at her desk and paged the ship's communication officer.

"I need you to send a transmission for me," she said. "To the Guild's High Council." The young man nodded, and turned to adjust several controls. She waited patiently until he finished, then spoke with a steady, somber voice into her view screen.

"I regret to inform you that Lord Von'hot of Von'hotten has formally expelled Guild leadership from his system," she said. "I cannot express the dismay I feel over this, and it is with grave sorrow that I must also tell you that Daniella Forester, a member of the Guild in good standing to this point, has opted to betray us and stay with him. I spoke with her myself, and am quite sure she is not being held against her will. We will, of course, have to take immediate action against Lord Von'hot, and perhaps appeal to the Emperor. I also recommend that we expel Daniella. She is a traitor to our organization, and should be treated as such."

Karya switched off the screen and sat back in her chair, eyes closed. *Take care, child,* she thought. She wished she could have stayed to ease things for Dani, but she knew from personal experience how hard it could be to be the mistress of a Von'hot lord. *Take care.*

Too Hot To Handle

A Northlanders Tale

Written by

Shelby Morgen

Chapter 1

"Come back to bed, M'Lady."

A stranger with an athletic build and possessive eyes sought to draw her back into his arms, but a commotion beyond the window distracted her. The noises that had awakened her were getting louder. Apparently pandemonium was breaking loose on the streets below. The man rose to cross the room to her, a dim figure in the shadows and lights that filtered through the curtains, his chest a washboard of carefully sculpted muscle that alternately glinted and darkened.

"Mmm." Strong hands with fingertips as smooth as a child's encircled her waist, brushing across her navel. He pulled her back against his outthrust cock, letting her feel its heat against her bare ass, then stroked his hands upward over her sensitive belly to capture her breasts. Her body responded almost involuntarily as he pinched at her traitorous nipples, rolling them gently between soft, knowing fingers.

Her head ached from the after-effects of too much ale, and there was a man she didn't remember pawing at her. Damn. She simply could not be trusted. *Who in the nine hells was he?*

"You have the body of a Warrior goddess. So tight

and firm." His fingers stroked over her clit as he rubbed his cock in slow circles against her ass. For a moment she feared he would try to gain entrance there. "So difficult to tame. You have been very disobedient, Slave. I fear I must punish you."

Last night came swirling back into focus. He'd worked very hard trying to convince her of his mastery. Unfortunately she hadn't been drunk enough to believe him capable of forcing her to do anything. Ever.

"Later," she warned. "I'm not in the mood at the moment." She hoped for his sake that he would take the hint. Such a pity to have to kill him. He was so pretty. At least she thought he was. She hadn't really seen him in the light of day…

"Feel how hard I am for you. You will come back to bed with me now, Slave. My cock wants you. Time to show me what an obedient slave you can be." He didn't add *this time,* but he didn't have to. "If you're very good, I'll fuck you until you scream."

Yeah. Right.

Jarla fought back the urge to peel his hands off her breasts. If she screamed it would be with frustration. She must not have paid the man, or he wouldn't still be here. She really shouldn't drink cheap ale. It did such bad things to her judgment.

The man bent to nuzzle her neck, letting his thick mass of dirty blond hair fall over her shoulder with a studied grace, obviously contrasting the blond of his hair with the dark burnt bronze of her skin. Suddenly he froze, his lips on her earlobe as he looked out the window over her shoulder.

Fires dotted the rooflines of thatched huts at the far end of town, racing to claim the marketplace, fanned by the cold north wind. Unable to damage the impenetrable stone walls of the city, the fire spread through the thatch-roofed wooden sheds in the Slaves' quarters with a destruction few invading enemies could have managed.

People were running from the market section in all directions, scattering like sheep before a pack of wild dogs.

"Do you think the fires will spread this far? Should we evacuate, M'Lady?"

The man—it really was coarse of her not to remember his name—sounded truly alarmed. Just short of panic. Jarla barely glanced at her consort as she pulled on her thin leather tunic, yanking her blackened ring mail over her head with a carelessness that ripped at her hair. "Evacuate?" The wind was blowing from the north—away from them. Still, 'twas a good enough way to get rid of him. "Aye. A good plan. Round up the others and see that they all make it out of this fine establishment."

"M'Lady?"

What had passed for strength and mastery last night now looked a shade too much like dumb as the stone the city was named for. "Much of this building is wood. If the fires spread it will go up like kindling. Go and knock on the doors of the other—

entertainers—who work here. Make sure everyone is awake and knows they must flee."

"But where will we go?" His deep voice rose close to a shriek as he pulled on his tunic.

"For now, take everyone to the river north of town. After the fires are under control I'm sure your master will see to finding you a new home. You are all too valuable to go homeless for long..." Damn it, he must have had a name. Jarla tossed a pair of gold coins to him. "Go."

He stared, wide eyed, at the coins in his hand for a moment. "Yes, M'Lady. I shall do as you instruct." He leaned in to kiss her quickly before he fled, although at the door he turned to look back over his shoulder. "Thank you, M'Lady!"

She couldn't get away from the tavern fast enough. *What is wrong with me?* she mused rather morosely as she took the outside stairs two at a time. The man was gorgeous. And he'd been talented enough. She simply wasn't able to convince herself that a man like that would ever master her. What was the point in playing sex games if you didn't believe the man was capable of outwitting you? There was no danger. No excitement. If all she had wanted was sex he would have been an admirable companion. But he had lacked the ability to make her believe for even an instant that she could not break him with one blow, had he ever truly frightened her.

The sex hadn't even been all that great. Not that the darling hadn't been eager to please her. But she hadn't wanted to be fawned over. She'd wanted strength. Passion. Mastery. She'd wanted, just for once, not to be the one in control—the one making all the decisions. A little ingenuity, damn it. Was that asking too much?

He'd been the prettiest of Stone City Tavern's offerings. Young and handsome and well endowed, his stamina had proved almost legendary. But sometimes a woman wanted more, wanted…

"By the gods," she whispered as she rounded the corner of the last set of stairs to run straight into the broadest chest she had ever had the pleasure of observing. She looked up, trying to see something beyond the massive chest. Up. And up. And up.

Strong hands shot out to steady her, lifting her easily off the ground. Lust hit her like a hard wave, knocking her breath from her lungs. She was no wisp of a woman. A man who could pick her up so easily could surely make her believe anything he wished. She kept looking up, wordlessly searching for his face.

The man's countenance went dead as he glanced down at her. His gaze dropped to focus respectfully at her feet as he set her back on the ground, though a muscle in his jaw went rock hard. "Forgive me, M'Lady."

The torc on his neck branded him a slave. Another wave of lust shot through her. A huge bear of a man who could break her with just one blow of those mighty hands, but instead was forced to serve her, submitting to her every whim. Ahh. This wasn't her usual fantasy, but surprisingly enough she found the idea even more arousing. Moisture flooded her sheath, quickly soaking the leather thong she wore beneath her leggings.

She reached out to touch, running her fingers through the short crisp curls that darkened the skin between his nipples. She let her palm glide across to stroke one of those inviting coral buds, pleased at his sharp intake of breath as it beaded up beneath her palm. "I would not have wasted my time with the pretty blond boy last night had I known there was a man about. Come upstairs with me, Slave. Now."

His eyes widened in surprise. "I am flattered, M'Lady, but—"

"Are you not a slave? Is it not your duty to obey me?"

"No, M'Lady. That is, I am a slave, but I do not work here. I am a fighter in the arena."

She struggled for her voice. She should have known. She had not even the effects of the ale to blame this time. She should have realized his torc was too realistically sculpted to be a bit of jewelry. It was the real thing. The raw scrape across his left shoulder suggested he had just escaped the fires. Jarla looked around him toward the Slaves' quarters. "The Arena? It is not closed this time of the year? Are there others?"

"M'Lady?"

Was he no brighter than the hireling? "Are there other men still trapped in the Slaves' quarters beneath the arena? Chained up in there so that they cannot escape?"

"Aye, M'Lady." He kept glancing over her shoulder, surveying the passageway beyond her as if he wanted to be on his way, to shove her aside, though he kept his hands hanging loosely at his sides.

A fire, panic in the streets, utter pandemonium. He wore a torc, yet he ran free while others stayed behind to suffer and die. Opportune timing? The twinges she'd felt in her loins moved higher, turning into the bile of disgust in her gut. "Don't let me stand in the way of your escape." Jarla sidestepped to allow him to pass as she headed for the burning buildings.

"I need a weapon, M'Lady." His voice was low, yet powerful, desperately asking her to believe in him. "I broke down the gates, but I could no' free them."

The hint of a brogue and his size branded him a Northlander. Jarla turned to stare at the huge bear of a man once again. "You expected to find weapons to free the Slaves in a whorehouse?"

"The *tavern* has kitchens, M'Lady. An axe for the firewood. A meat cleaver. Anything."

A Northlander? Here? There could be only one reason for a Northlander to venture into these parts. Especially one wearing a slave's torc. After all these months…

But he was attempting to free the Slaves. Without help they would all die, slowly suffocating on the smoke long before the flames began to crackle about their feet.

She was a professional, damn it. The job came first. Always.

She was a fool.

Jarla closed her eyes for the barest of moments, asking the gods' forgiveness for her stupidity. She tossed her axe to the man with the pleading eyes. She noted that his fingers were raw and bloody, as if he'd tried to rip the chains apart with his bare hands, yet he grinned as he caught her axe. "I thank ye, M'Lady."

And with that he was gone.

His long, ragged black hair flew out behind him as he raced back towards the burning stables. The stables connected to the arena. Damn it. There must be a dozen ways out of the arena. Jarla laughed at the surprise on the big man's face as she passed him, then stopped to wait for him to catch up as she armed herself with her short sword.

He didn't question her reason for being here, nor her ability to deal with danger. He simply accepted the strip of cloth she offered and tied it over his face as he led the way through the billowing smoke.

Damn but she liked the look of this man. Too bad he hadn't been the one sharing her bed last night instead of that fancy little piece of rent-a-cock. She was willing to bet she wouldn't have ended the night so disappointed.

Once past the entrance to the stables it was harder to breathe. Without the big man in front of her, judging every turn with apparent confidence, she would quickly have become disoriented in this maze of a building. The smoke swirled around them, obscuring everything but her view of the big man's backside as they pushed forward. Damn. She was chasing the man through a burning building and all she could think about was the lovely piece of prime meat about to go up in smoke. She'd been alone way too much recently. But since from the look of things she was about to end up roasted, there wasn't too much harm in enjoying her very last look.

A fine ass it was, too.

Jarla admonished herself once again as she nearly ran into that fine, tight ass. She'd been too busy studying the play of muscles over his back as he moved to notice when he stopped suddenly. She swallowed her laughter. What a shame she'd maintained her balance. She'd have kept her hands where they landed, caressing the curves of his hips, but his attention was focused on other things.

He raised her axe to splinter a large wooden door. Once inside he led her down a set of crude wooden stairs to a sweltering dungeon. The air was rank with the smell of human waste. Her laughter died on her lips.

The smoke hadn't thoroughly penetrated this far below ground yet. They yanked the cloths from over their faces. The air was clear enough for her to see the wasted lumps of humanity chained along the wall like a herd of tethered goats. Evidently the slave trader had been working overtime of late.

A chain passed through the torc on each man's neck then through an iron ring bolted to the wall. At either end of the row the chain was padlocked to the last man's torc.

Her guide paused before the first man in the line. "I am sorry, Calibeth." His voice was far from steady.

"Do it," the gray form barked. He closed his eyes and turned toward the wall. "Grant me my freedom, Thallin. Do it!"

Thallin. Her guess had been correct. By the seven. What was he doing *here*? More important, what was he going to do with—

An axe for the firewood. A meat cleaver. Anything.

"No!" Jarla screamed as the big man raised her axe above his head. "Stop! Thallin, stop!" She cringed as she threw herself in front of Calibeth. "You don't have to do this, Thallin," she tried to explain.

She felt the prisoner's hands on her waist, shoving her out of the way as she fished in her small leather waist pouch. "Fool woman, do you think this is easy for him? Can you not see that we will all die here? Let him do his work!"

The prisoner knocked her off balance, and as she stumbled her tools scattered to the ground. "No, no, you don't understand. Just give me a moment!"

As Thallin stared at her, the axe fell slowly to the ground. He dropped to his knees, shaking hands reaching for her tools as tears streamed down his face. "By the gods," he croaked out in a mockery of laughter. "These are lock picks. She's a thief."

"A Mercenary," Jarla corrected automatically. "At the moment I'm working as a Bounty Hunter." Thallin's sun-bronzed face paled as she snatched her tools out of his hands. "Thank you."

Unaware of what passed between them, the prisoner stretched his neck and turned his head, giving her as much room to work as he could. "The gods are with us this night," he breathed. "Our prayers are twice answered."

Jarla didn't have time to wonder what the older man meant. She'd worry over that later. For now there was a Dwarven lock under her fingers.

"Can I fetch ye anything?" Thallin offered. "Do ye need a light?"

"No!" she snapped, her concentration broken. "Just be quiet." Instantly the slave pit took on the quiet of a tomb. She'd have sworn the men ceased to breathe.

'Twas no use. The Dwarven lock refused to budge. Yet she couldn't give up. She couldn't let Thallin use her axe to…

A soft click sounded under her hands. "One," she muttered.

The smoke was getting thicker down here. The

roof above must be caving in. Would she set the men free only to have them all roasted alive?

Her hands held steady on her tools. Another soft snap. "Two."

"Now you're so damn quiet you're breaking my concentration. Breathe, damn it."

The prisoner beneath her hands chuckled. "If that isn't just like a woman. Give 'em exactly what they ask for and what do you get? Nothing but complaints."

A thin trickle of laughter echoed down the line. Jarla laughed with them, her tension dissipating. One more small push, and the lock fell open in her hands. "Three!"

To her surprise, the wasted-looking prisoner picked her up and spun her about, hugging her once before he tossed her to Thallin. Hastily the others began yanking the chain back through the rings, each man helping the next.

Thallin snatched her out of the air and crushed her against his chest. "I am forever in thy debt, Bounty Hunter," he whispered against her ear.

"You can repay me by getting us all out of here alive."

"Aye. That I can."

But he didn't put her down. Instead he kissed her, making a show of nuzzling her lips and her neck. His words were urgent, but too soft to carry beyond her ears. "I beg of ye, do not let the men know why ye are here. They would fight to protect me. They are too weak. Someone would get hurt." He kissed her again, feasting on her lips like a starving man. "I will no' try to escape. I give ye my word."

She was standing face to face with the man she'd been tracking for six months, surrounded by a score of freed prisoners, in a burning building, about to be roasted to death, and the world ceased to exist outside of that kiss. His tongue swept her lips like a starving man feasting on succulent delights. How long had it been since she'd met a man with fire, with passion, with the strength to turn her into a quivering ball of need with just the touch of his lips?

A cheer echoed through the chamber, reminding them of where they were. Thallin released his hold on her, letting her slide slowly down his chest until her feet hit the floor. There was no mistaking the hard, jutting bulge beneath his brief waistcloth. By the gods. From the feel of things, he was big *everywhere*. Her hands tangled in his hair to drag his head down to her level. Another cheer filled the stone chamber as she nipped at his lip, then ran her tongue over the wound.

"Please, M'Lady."

Her breath hitched in her throat. "Swear you will do whatever I demand of you."

Thallin ran the tip of his tongue over the cleft in her chin to catch a bead of sweat that formed there. "Anything," he agreed as he pulled away reluctantly.

Jarla had the grace to blush as she turned to

survey the men. The man on the other end of the chain was, of course, still attached to roughly thirty-odd feet of heavy iron links, but the others held the chain now like a lifeline, supporting its weight and using it as a way to keep in contact once they reached the upper level. "Let's get the hells out of here, men," she urged. "I believe we all have better things to do."

The men laughed again. Thallin nodded once, then took off through the thickening smoke.

Jarla fell to her knees, gasping in lungfuls of moderately clean air. They hadn't come out at all where she'd expected. They were in the arena, not back at the gates near the tavern. The gates that allowed the public to enter the arena—the gates Thallin had broken down with his shoulder—were all that stood between the Slaves and freedom. The men separated, seeking out whatever arms and equipment they could find in the debris. Jarla moved to the man who still bore the chain as soon as she caught her breath, beating the second Dwarven lock more easily now that she'd mastered the first.

"Go," Thallin ordered. "Argolyn will be back all too soon with the prisoners who staged the escape. Ye must be far away when he returns."

"We go," Calibeth agreed. "We will take refuge at the Dwarven Monastery until we are strong enough to return to our homes. Argolyn dare not pursue us there. His own people have exiled him for his traitorous ways."

Thallin clasped the arm Calibeth extended.

"Come with us," Calibeth offered. "You know you will be welcome wherever we travel."

"I canna'." Something unspoken passed between the men. Thallin raised his head toward the mountains, and the tundra beyond. "My way lies north. Fear not. I will no' travel alone. Safe journey to ye, friends."

"Safe journey."

Neither Thallin nor Jarla spoke until the men were out of sight. It was Thallin who finally broke the silence. He spoke without looking at her, once again dropping the axe from his bloodied fingers. "Let us be about our business, Bounty Hunter. We canna' stand here all day pretending ye have no' a job to do."

"Aye," Jarla agreed with a sigh. She pulled the hobbles and wrist cuffs out of her bag as she began her familiar routine. "Thallin MacCalla, I hereby place you under arrest for the murder of Jonas McDevlin."

Chapter 2

Thallin said nothing as he allowed her to strap the cuffs around him. The wrist cuffs came nowhere near fitting, so she had to use the hobbles on his wrists, and pray that he wouldn't run. She wanted to believe he would not. He could have killed her a dozen times in the tunnels out to the arena. Instead he had kissed her. Kissed her like no man had before.

"It is not my place to judge you nor punish you. It is my duty to return you to the Northlands, that you may stand trial for your crime."

"Ye have already shown me much more kindness than I expected from one of thy kind," Thallin assured her. "I am ready to go home."

"I must collect my bags. We will go back to the tavern first."

"As ye will, M'Lady," he agreed. If he was thinking of the greeting she'd met him with some hours ago he did not speak of it.

The tavern remained untouched by the fires, though if the wind shifted, sparks could conceivably catch its thatched roof on fire, sending it up in flames with the rest of the poorer sections of town. But for now it was safe enough.

And empty.

Every fiber of Jarla's being hummed with her awareness of the bound man following so closely behind her as she climbed the stairs to her room. Thallin looked capable enough of killing a man. He wouldn't even need a weapon. He was strong enough to strangle a man with his bare hands. But he didn't look vicious. He stood silently next to the bed, awaiting her orders. His hard bronze body streaked with sweat and ash from the fire, his long black hair ragged and wild, and his hands manacled with her sturdy leather hobbles, he looked dangerous enough to leave her hot and wanting.

There were many things Jarla prided herself on. Self-restraint was not one of them. She gathered her things back into her pack and stood it next to the door before she turned to face the big man, knowing he would see the lust burning in her eyes. Knowing and wanting him to see. His nostrils flared as she stepped closer to him, but still he said nothing.

"You swore you would do anything I asked of you," Jarla reminded him. "Will you stand by that promise?"

His body trembled at her nearness. "Aye," he repeated, his voice husky. "Anything."

Lust shot through her veins, making them sing with need and desire. "We need not leave for the Northlands just this moment. Already the day is well gone." She dampened a scrap of toweling in the washbasin next to the bed and lifted it to wash the scrapes on his shoulder. He flinched at her touch. "Do not move," she admonished as she ran the cool water over the reddened skin. "Never have I harmed a prisoner in my custody."

"Then why do ye torture me so, M'Lady?"

"Your wound needs tended."

"'Tis not all that needs tended."

Jarla tried to stifle her smile, but it was no use. "You have other injuries?" she asked, playing along with his banter.

"Aye, M'Lady. I fear the wound is near mortal. Surely if ye do not tend to me I shall die."

Jarla ran her hands over him, examining every inch of him carefully. His back felt broad and strong and apparently undamaged. His ass—that perfect ass she'd admired as she followed him through the smoke-filled stables—was still just as perfect. His breath drew in sharply as she checked all the surfaces of that ass, letting her fingers pause to spread the cheeks and circle close to the tightly puckered opening. His cheeks clenched, almost involuntarily, though his ass shoved back against her hands.

"So far everything feels just fine," she assured the giant before her. "Where do you hurt?"

"Everywhere," he managed in a choked whisper.

Jarla brought her hands down over his hips to the long, hard length of his thighs, then up, feathering the fine hair that grew along the insides of his legs above his knees. He was trembling by the time her hands slipped under his waistcloth. "I have never mistreated a prisoner," she reminded him.

The waistcloth jumped and bobbed before her, though her hands hadn't moved. "I will let ye know should ye mistreat me, M'Lady. I will ask ye to desist."

So, he understood the rules of the game. *Desist* was to be their safe word then. "I cannot have you escaping."

He thrust himself urgently at her hands. "I would sooner die that escape ye, M'Lady."

"You say that now. But later we will sleep. And if you should wake up before me, then what?"

"I might attempt to distract ye from thy mission yet a while longer."

He might. And then again she might spend another six months tracking him down. Jarla fished in her bags for the set of too small wrist cuffs. "Lie down on the bed."

He did as she ordered, though a fine sheen of sweat broke out on his jaw. "Yes, M'Lady. As you command."

Jarla looped the chain from the cuffs around the bedpost, then fastened the two cuffs together, making one larger band which she buckled around his left wrist, stretching his hand far above his head. His eyes—large, luminescent green eyes—watched her every move with a strange mixture of both fear and desire. He swallowed hard, but said nothing.

He didn't fight her until she reached his right ankle. Then, as if suddenly realizing what she was about, he jerked his ankle out from under her hand, a wild, frightened look in his eyes. Jarla backed away. Moving beyond his reach she slowly removed her ring mail, folding it carefully onto the chair beside the nightstand. Next came the leggings and soft leather undertunic. Last came the small leather thong, a dark stain spreading across its pale gray surface. By the time she was naked, his breathing was hard, and he rubbed his ass slowly against the hard, knobby surface of the bedspread.

She turned to him, using the torn toweling to clear away the grime of the day. His gaze riveted to the spot where the cool water trickled between her breasts.

"I have never harmed a prisoner," she reminded the big man. She moved back to the bedside to run her fingers across his chest, gently tweaking the hard points of his nipples so that he moaned with desire. "I've never fucked a prisoner before, either."

"Let me touch," he begged.

"I've got to cuff you."

"Aye, M'Lady. I know. Ye have no reason to trust me."

"It is you who have no reason to trust me. And therein lies the danger."

He began to sweat again as she reached for his ankle. "I—please do not, M'Lady. I give you my word."

Jarla ran her hands over the leg she meant to bind, trying to calm him. When he jerked free, she backed away, crossing her arms over her chest. "Did you kill him? Did you murder Jonas McDevlin?"

Fierce passion returned to his eyes, supplanting the fear. "Oh, aye, I killed him. The bloody bastard. But I would no' call it murder."

There was really nothing holding him now, nothing but the one wrist cuff. If he but rolled away from her, he could have that off in moments. "Lady Ayailla sends you a message. She says you are a good man, and that it is time to put your faith in the laws of your people."

He closed his eyes, a look of pain crossing his face. "Aye. The Lady is wise."

"And she trusts me. Do you?" Jarla moved quickly, not waiting for his answer. Before he could register her intent, she slipped the cuff around his ankle and buckled it tightly in place, drawing his leg and arm taught diagonally across the bed. He would still be able to move, but there was no way he could bring the free hand to the bound wrist.

Unless, of course, he managed to tear apart the bed. With a mighty roar Thallin flung himself into the air, attempting to break the bedposts with his own body weight. Jarla jumped atop him, tangling her hands in his hair as she held on for her life. The eyes that looked up at her were the eyes of an animal, wild and unreasoning, filled with rage and fear. He lunged at her, his teeth snapping, all trace of humanity gone.

"Thallin! Thallin, listen to me!" she cried. "Thallin, I will not hurt you. *Thallin*!"

Slowly he calmed beneath her weight and her restraining hands, though he turned his head away, refusing to meet her gaze. "If I wanted to hurt ye, I could have done so long before this. *Desist*, M'Lady."

His voice sounded angry and bitter. Jarla stretched to cover the cuff on his wrist with her hand. "This is not a part of our games, Thallin. This is my job. I do what I have to do, what I am paid to do. If you escape me, I may well be forced to spend the next six months tracking you down again. The choice to trust you or not is not mine to make. Surely you understand what it is to follow a duty. You would have killed your friend out of duty, that the others might be freed. All I ask of you now is that you tolerate this one simple restraint. Can you not bear this for me?"

She stroked her hands over his arms and chest as she spoke, using the feel of her skin and the sound of her voice to bring him back to her. At last he turned to look at her again. "For ye, M'Lady. And for the debt I owe Calibeth. But ye must understand. I escaped the Slavers weeks ago. I returned now only to free my friends. I will not go back there again. Give me thy word that should the Dwarf Argolyn and his men return, ye will not let them take me alive."

It was captivity he feared—or perhaps the Dwarf himself. "I will not let the Dwarf recapture you," Jarla promised.

His gaze searched her face. "That is not what I asked of ye, M'Lady."

Jarla swallowed hard. "I have never yet lost a prisoner. But should the Dwarf find us, I will not let you be captured alive."

His free hand moved to touch her, brushing her hair back from her face, pulling her head down so that he could taste her lips, sucking the bottom one into his mouth like a piece of hard candy. "I do not believe ye will lose this prisoner, either, M'Lady. I believe ye are good at thy job. Good enough to see me safely home. Ye are the most beautiful Bounty Hunter I have ever seen, M'Lady. And perhaps the most deadly."

His free leg snaked out to press her hips hard against his. She responded by kneading her hands into his shoulders, rolling her hips down over the length of his neglected cock. The fear had only made him harder, hotter. She squeezed her thighs together, holding him trapped between their bodies, caressing his hot length with the muscles of her butt. He groaned, sounding like a wounded animal, reaching his right arm around her to search for the nipple that remained just out of his reach.

Jarla sat up to give him a better view. "You are my prisoner," she reminded him.

He tested his restraints, then licked his lips slowly, as if remembering the game. "Yes, M'Lady."

She raised her hands to stroke them slowly over her breasts, lifting and shaping them until the nipples stood out like two erect points of desire. "You will refer to me as Mistress."

"Yes, Mistress."

"You have sworn to obey my commands."

"I will do whatever ye demand of me, Mistress."

But what could she do with a bound, helpless man? She ached everywhere, already hungry for his touch, but her duty prohibited her what she wanted most.

Or did it?

"Suck me," she hissed, bending forward until her breast was a few inches away from his mouth.

His lips curved back into a smile. "Yes, Mistress."

He lunged to catch her in his mouth. The first swipe of his tongue around the areola had her shuddering with desire. Uninvited, his hand moved to her other breast, stroking, teasing, encouraging her to press herself against his hand. He worked the hard bud of her nipple against the backs of his teeth, rolling and twisting both his tongue and her nipple until she thrust at him mindlessly, her desire escaping in a long, low moan.

Jarla pulled away, needing to catch her breath, wanting to maintain control. "Did I give you permission to touch me?"

"No, Mistress. I apologize. I shall accept thy punishment."

He looked far too pleased with himself.

Jarla stroked her breasts, everywhere but over the tips that wanted so badly to be touched. And why shouldn't they be? She licked her fingertips, rubbing them slowly over the hard, needy nipples.

His eyelids dropped to half shut, and his breathing became labored again as he watched. "Please, Mistress."

"Please what?"

"I want to touch ye. I need to touch ye."

"But this isn't about what you want, is it?"

"No, Mistress," he agreed.

"You may touch yourself."

Staring at her, his eyes aflame with white-hot desire, he dropped his hand to slide it between them, capturing his cock and using the tip to mimic the action of her fingers where they outlined her nipples. She felt the hot, wet drops of his fluids mingling with her already flowing juices. Could she actually reach orgasm just watching a man pleasure himself?

Jarla placed one hand over his, encouraging, urging, demanding more as he teased and aroused her. Their hands linked together around his cock, driving her fingers to more adventurous tweaking of her nipples, first one, and then the other.

She wanted more. She wanted…

She could have whatever she wanted. She raised his hand from his cock to her breast. With a quick prayer to the gods that she could hold him, she lowered her dripping sheath onto his cock.

He froze, not moving a muscle as she squirmed slightly, adjusting herself around him, sinking slowly over his throbbing shaft, letting her body stretch to accommodate him. So hot. So full. She placed her hand over his on her breast, lowering herself fully onto him.

She was the one whose breath came in ragged gasps now. She rose over him, then dropped down harder, experimenting, trying the fit out for size. She felt him shudder within her, could see the strain of his restraint standing out in a thin line of sweat pooling along his upper lip. She wiggled experimentally. He bit his lip to keep from crying out.

"Mistress," he pleaded.

"Yes, Slave? Is there something you want?"

"Mistress, let me touch ye. Let me—"

"No." Perhaps because he wanted it, perhaps to prove her control, she removed his hand from her breast. He fisted his hand in the sheets, sobbing in frustration. She bent down to kiss him, rubbing her tits across his chest, riding his length as she did so. When she sat up again she came down hard, riding the wave of sensation as she stretched to accommodate his full girth.

That felt good. Better than anything she'd felt for a long time. She wanted more. She rose up again and dropped back, grinding against him as he filled her completely, driving him into her harder and deeper this time.

More. She wanted more. She wasn't sure if she'd said so aloud, but he knew. His hand steadied her as he shifted his hips beneath her, setting rhythm to the dance as he slid in and out of her, gently at first, then stronger. She braced herself with one hand on his chest, clenched over the hard bud of his nipple, kneading, clawing, demanding.

Their mating took on a rhythm of its own, rough and unrelenting, their breath coming in frenzied gasps as they clawed at each other, fingers probing, bodies driving together in wild abandon. She screamed as she clamped down on him, her muscles tightening with sweet release, and yet still it was not enough. He rose into her time and again, driving her past her endurance. She came again, her voice a shrieking wail as she sobbed out his name.

"Now, Thallin!" she demanded as she clenched around him. "Now!"

His tempo increased to a frenzied pounding that shattered her yet again as his seed shot into her with a hot rush, spurting hard and full as she milked him for more. "Yes, Mistress," he groaned as he quivered within her, his body still jerking uncontrollably with the aftershocks of their culmination.

His voice was soft, so soft she had to strain to hear him over the loud beating of his heart under her ear. "Ye need not these chains to hold me, Mistress. My word holds me more strongly than chains ever could. Let me touch ye. Let me hold ye. I will no' try to escape. I will no'. Ye have my word."

She was seven kinds of a fool. But she was too sated to argue with him. She reached above her head without opening her eyes to fumble with his wrist cuff. When at last it came undone, his arms closed around her, cradling her, as he rolled her to his side. Sleep pulled at her, opening its welcoming arms, seducing her with its warm nothingness. "Do not leave me," she whispered.

"No, Mistress. I gave ye my word. I could no' if I wanted to. And I am no' such a fool."

She fell asleep to the steady, reassuring beat of his heart beneath her ear and the welcome feel of his cock still buried deep within her.

Chapter 3

The room was awash with the dull glow of the first light of dawn. Jarla turned to snuggle against the warmth of Thallin's body, but there was nothing there. She sobbed in defeat as she rolled her face into the empty place in the bed where he had lain.

She'd known. 'Twas no one's fault but her own. What fool would wait for her to take him to trial when he could be free? 'Twas not just the ale that affected her judgment. Apparently 'twas any warm male body. She pounded her fist into the mattress in frustration.

What was wrong with her? Was she so depraved in her longings that she had allowed her pleasure to interfere with her work? If word of this got out she would be the laughingstock of the guild. She would never be able to show her face in the Northlands again. By the seven, she would catch him, and she would punish him for his breach of her trust. She would—

Thallin swept her up into his arms as if she were but a tiny Elfling. "Good morning, Mistress." He kissed her as if he had the right to do so, and she did not bother to object. She was so relieved that she wound her arms around him, burying her hands in his hair.

He slid her down the length of his body until her feet just barely touched the floor. "Are ye hungry, Mistress?"

"Aye," she agreed, though they both knew she was not thinking about bread and cheese, or even a leftover slab of roast boar. He kissed her again, one hand sliding down her back to press her hips against his, letting her know she was not the only one who hungered, while the other tangled itself in the heavy mass of her hair. "Starving."

He chuckled as he scooped her up into his arms again, only to deposit her gently in the large copper bathtub. "I will feed ye after we bathe." He must have been hauling water to fill the thing for at least the last hour. 'Twas no small job, even for one with a body like his, hauling buckets of water from the pump in the courtyard, but he managed it before she had opened her eyes.

"You could have been miles from here by now," she mused. "Yet you stayed. Why?"

"I gave ye my word."

Perhaps for him it was as simple as that.

Who had ever known a bath could be so erotic? But with the huge man on his knees beside her, running the soft cloth over her breasts, pausing to polish her nipples until she thought they might explode with desire, the water trailing down over her belly, she could think of nothing more erotic.

Unless it was those hands, strong enough to end a man's life, gently untangling her hair with a bristled brush he'd managed to acquire. Or those same hands placing a towel over the tub's rim for padding, bending her head back so that he could lower her hair into a separate tub as he washed the mass of it. Or perhaps it was his fingers, massaging her scalp, easing her tensions away. Her eyes slid shut.

When he stopped, she opened her eyes, looking up at him in sudden bereavement.

"What do ye want from me, Mistress?"

She stared at him, unable to comprehend what he was asking.

"Ye came here, to this place—this tavern—looking for something. If ye had found it, ye would be about the bounty that brought ye here, instead of lying abed with me."

"Your trail had grown cold," she admitted. "I was lonely…"

"Ye have had other lovers," he mused. "But they left ye wanting."

"Yes," she agreed, too far gone to argue against the truth.

"There is much more to owning a slave than controlling him with chains," he promised. "What is the use of owning a slave if ye still do all the work? Let me show ye. Let me teach ye. I will no' leave ye lonely."

Words like *duty* and *honor* plagued her. They

should be far from here by now, well on the road to the Northlands.

No one had paid her to find this man. There was no fee unless she returned him. She had made no promises as to when she would bring him back. Her time was her own. Jarla smiled slowly as she settled back into the water. "Teach me, Slave. Make me regret not neglecting my duties more often."

He laughed as his bathing moved lower, the scrap of toweling gently parting her folds, his fingers stroking below the water until she splashed water out of the tub as she writhed against him. In moments her fires burned as high as they had yester eve, her need so strong she thought she might die of unfulfilled lust. He brought her almost to her peak, so close, so close, then withdrew, only to start again, then again. She wanted to scream with frustration and pent-up desire.

Next he lifted her to her feet, standing her in the tub while he rinsed her and dried her with a larger square of toweling. He laid her back on a pile of pillows atop the bed, her head raised enough that she might watch as he stepped into the tub. Slowly, with the grace of an artist, he washed the sweat and soot from his body. She felt herself growing wet and needy again as she watched.

By the time he finished she was ready to devour him on the spot. But he was not done. With his hands, he urged her to turn over, lying face down in the pillows. She almost changed her mind as he moved to straddle her hips, but he did not try to force his huge cock into her tiny opening. Instead he bent forward to rest his hands lightly on her shoulders. "Relax," he whispered. "I know how to please my Mistress."

"Aye," she agreed as his fingers began to knead gently into her shoulders. "Indeed." He worked tirelessly until her muscles were reduced to formless masses of pacified nerves, and then his strokes changed. He had found a bottle of oil somewhere—she vaguely remembered a drawer filled with toys and accessories. He smoothed the oil into her skin now, with long sweeping strokes down the length of her back, over her sides, and around ever closer to her breasts. His cock pressed closer to her anus with each stroke, its wet tip brushing against her as he bent, as if asking permission to enter.

Frightened, but too aroused to refuse him, she reached back to spread herself open, but it appeared he had other plans. One well-oiled finger searched out her opening, circling, probing, and finally slipping inside. He held still within her for a long moment, then gently forced his finger in farther.

"Breathe," he reminded her. "Ye must remember to breathe, Mistress."

She drew in her breath in a long searching pull that sent her muscles spasming against his finger. She nearly screamed from the sweet mixture of pleasure and pain. "I want..."

"Yes, Mistress?"

She raised her hips off the bed, shoving them up

invitingly at him. "I need to feel you. Inside me."

He withdrew his finger, only to replace it with what felt like three extremely large pearls knotted a few inches apart on a string. The pearls hummed, vibrating as she adjusted to the feel of them.

Before she could protest the intrusion—or decide if she really wanted to—he lifted her, rolling her to face him, her thighs spread wide, her body an offering before him. "So beautiful," he murmured. "So strong. So powerful. My Warrior Mistress."

She wanted to tell him that she was not beautiful, that she was too tall, too broad of shoulder, too dark, built too much like a man. But the lust shining in his eyes forced her to hold her tongue.

Thallin spread his hands against her belly, where she could see them, his darkly tanned skin still pale against hers. "So different. Exotic. What clan are ye? I have never seen a Human of such coloring or so exquisitely built."

She steeled herself for his rejection. "I have no clan. My father was Bear Clan. A slave in Élahandara. My mother was the half-breed offspring of an Élandra and a Human slave."

Thallin merely laughed. "Clan of the Wolf welcomes *Lobos*. We would make beautiful cubs together, all with thy exotic beauty."

Cubs? Children? He was already planning their children? She had not even—she could not—he was to be tried for murder, and she would be back to her own life, alone again...

He stopped her words before she could voice them, started with her mouth, with a kiss that made her forget what she might have objected to, then kissing and nipping his way down to her chin, paying special attention to the small dimple in its center. She'd never thought the underside of her jaw line especially sensitive, but with his hands on her, lifting her head, tilting her neck to expose more of her throat to his kisses, she felt her body fairly hum with desire.

She arched her chest against him, wanting his attentions to move lower still, but he was not ready to move on to her breasts just yet. Her collarbone held erogenous zones? She would not have thought so, but when he stopped to kiss the small knob near her shoulder she found herself twisting under him, anxious for more of his touch. His hands were busy as well, stroking over the length of her arms to link with her fingers, holding her pinned to the bed. She was his prisoner now, bound by the sheer size and weight of him, and more so by the force of her own desires.

Moving slowly, he brushed his nipples over her breasts, the friction between them light as the touch of a butterfly's wings. She would have pushed back against him more firmly, demanded more, but his hold on her hands allowed her too little freedom of movement. He brought her fingers to his mouth, suckling each finger separately before he brought her hand down to feel the rigid length of his cock where it twitched against his belly, already wet with his own pre-cum. He groaned aloud as together they stroked over his length.

"Fuck me," Jarla ordered. "Now."

"As ye command, Mistress."

Jarla expected him to thrust into her, especially after her direct order, but he did not. Instead he stroked his hands up her thighs, pausing to admire her wet, swollen flesh with a too pleased look of self-satisfaction before he lowered his mouth to suckle her clit.

Damn arrogant male. How dare he look at her with that self-satisfied gleam in his eyes? How dare he speak to her of the children they would not have? Did he think her some young neophyte, to be impressed by his strength and his willingness to obey her commands? Granted, he'd made her body respond to him, had her blood boiling to the point of desire that was near pain, but that did not make him so different. Other men had managed as much. Other men had—

His tongue thrust deep within her, reaching places untouched by the dim memories of past encounters. No other man had ever managed to bring her to the brink of orgasm with one thrust of his tongue. She cried out, fisting her hands in his hair as she bucked up against his probing tongue. He withdrew, only to thrust in again, his coarse, rough tongue lapping the walls of her vagina like some delectable treat.

His hands were busy as well, clever fingers

stroking as they held her open, riding beside her clit as she thrust herself against him.

Jarla screamed. She knew she was coming—there was no way to stop it, the sensations rocketing through her like an electric shock—and still she had not held him inside her. Her call came again as he stroked directly over her clit with the tip of his tongue, pausing between strokes to blow hot, moist breath over her.

"Now!" she ordered. "I want ye inside me now!"

Thallin reached for something he had left laying on the table beside the bed. Her eyes widened in surprise as he placed it in her palm. It was a polished ivory ring, with small nubs scattered over its edges. He was going to fit that—in addition to a penis the size of his—within her?

Apparently he did not share her lack of confidence. He guided her hand, showing her how to slide the ring down slowly over the length of his rigid, trembling cock. His eyes closed, and his fingers held her hand steady for a moment as the ring moved as far down over his shaft as it would go. His breath hissed out slowly.

"What is it? What does it do?" she couldn't help but ask.

"'Tis called a—a pleasure ring," he explained as coherently as he could manage.

A pleasure ring? Whose pleasure? It looked more painful than pleasurable. "How does it work?"

Thallin gave a final push, trembling beneath her hand as the ring slid the last inch to fit in place at the base of his penis. "It—they—delay my pleasure, as it enhances thine," he explained, his voice betraying his slipping control.

He placed two more rings in her hand. She frowned as she slid them over his penis, spacing them evenly apart. "They look painful. Perhaps they are not big enough for someone of your build," she worried. "How will we get them off?"

"They fit correctly," he assured her with a groan as she examined her handiwork, inspecting him carefully. He jerked beneath her fingers in anticipation. "They will come off easier, Mistress, once ye have made use of them."

"Show me," she ordered.

Ever the obedient slave, he lifted her knees, hooking them over his elbows as he knelt before her, shivering despite the warmth of the room as he pushed slowly into her.

She could feel the nubs of the rings as they slid into her. Her muscles clenched hard around him, more than ready to continue where they had left off. But the true use of the rings, she discovered, was in the sensation they made as he slowly withdrew from her.

Jarla screamed as the rings pulled out of her, each one producing a sucking pop. His next thrust was deeper, faster, as his body shook with the force of his lust. Still he slowed his pace as he withdrew. The orgasm clawed at her, so close, just slightly beyond her reach. She clawed at him, wordlessly demanding more. He laughed in triumph as he bucked into her, maintaining his slow, steady pace as the room began to grow dark around her. She gasped for breath, suddenly afraid of what was to come. She shook like a child's toy as he drove into her.

Another stroke. The slow, sensuous withdraw. Then another. She couldn't breathe. She fought him now, screaming as the world narrowed down to that one small area of contact between them, so sensitized that she could feel each ring as it raked against her defenseless flesh. His movements built up speed, his control slipping. She pulled at him now, desperate to make him come, desperate to come herself, yet afraid of something so intense, so—

Earth-shattering. The room went completely black. Her pulse pounded in her ears like the crash of waves against the rocks. She had never before lost consciousness, but surely this must be what it would feel like. She was falling, and there was no one to catch her.

No one but Thallin, his strong arms cradling her against his chest, his cock still rock hard within her. Thallin. Waiting patiently for her, his own lust unfulfilled. Thallin, who had shown her a new world.

Thallin. Whom she would repay by forcing him to return to stand trial for the murder of some man who probably desperately needed to die.

None of those things seemed to bother Thallin at

the moment. As the light returned to the room, he began to move within her again, faster this time, harder, driving her toward climax more quickly, until she shattered around him again, and yet again. She screamed out his name as she broke. "Now, Thallin. Come for me, Thallin. *Now*!"

She had thought her body could sustain no more sensation, but as he began to erupt within her in slow, intense waves that left him shaking violently in her arms, he still maintained the presence of mind to remember her beads. He pulled gently, drawing them out one at a time as she screamed his name over and over again.

Later. She would worry about Lady Ayailla later. The room went black again as she collapsed into his arms.

He was with her when she awoke this time. Sunlight flooded the room. She moved her head to snuggle closer in his arms. "We have a long journey ahead of us, Mistress," he whispered near her ear.

"I do not wish to make this journey, Thallin."

He stroked her hair, kissing her once on the top of her head. "I have no wish to spend the rest of my life running from my past, M'Lady. It is time to go home."

She pressed her ear against his chest, listening to the steady beat of his heart, her eyes damp with unshed tears. "I need to know, Thallin. Why did you kill Jonas McDevlin?"

He lay quiet beside her for a moment too long. "It is not a pretty story, M'Lady."

"Death rarely is."

His voice came softly, so that she had to strain to listen. "Jonas and I were in love with the same woman. She chose me. After we married, Jonas' hatred of me built until he could not stand to see me succeed in anything. His raiders stole my stock. His men poisoned my water. Finally he kidnapped my wife. She would no' go with him willingly, so he raped her and killed her. When I caught up with him I strangled him with my bare hands."

Hands that had been so gentle with her. Jarla captured one of those hands to bring it to her lips. "What will happen when I take you home, Thallin?"

"I will stand before the Tribunal. 'Tis just a formality really."

"And?"

"And when the charges are read, I will plead guilty."

She swallowed hard. "Would it do no good to plead your cause, Thallin?"

"I took another man's life, M'Lady. 'Twas not my place to do so, no matter the cause. Retribution is the domain of the courts."

"What—what retribution will those courts extract from you?"

"I have sacrificed my right to freedom, M'Lady. I will spend the rest of my days in bondage. In all likelihood I will be sold to the Dwarves who mine the mountains below Élahandara. The money from my sale will go to Jonas' family."

She had suspected as much. Jarla quieted the voice that called her a fool. "Could someone else, someone other than the Dwarves—Thallin, could I buy your bond?"

He kept his voice carefully controlled. "Aye, M'Lady. Anyone with enough gold pieces could buy my bond."

Jarla pushed far enough away from him to be able to see his eyes. "I would not be allowed to free you. You would wear my torc about your neck for the rest of your life. Would you want this? To be my slave outside the bedroom?"

"I will not go cheaply, M'Lady. What is the price of a man's life?"

A great deal more than the price of his bounty, Jarla wagered. "That was not my question," she reprimanded gently.

Hope flared in his beautiful green eyes. "Aye, M'Lady. Nothing would please me more."

Jarla rolled out of bed to reach for her clothes. "If the Dwarf Argolyn returns, I shall purchase your bond from him as well."

"'Tis said Argolyn placed himself between a powerful Shaman and her mate. I do not believe he will return, M'Lady."

Jarla laughed. "A woman would do much to

defend her mate."

"And a man his."

"Aye," she agreed as she let him assist her with her armor. "Tell me again about these children we will have."

He kissed her as he adjusted the ring mail over her shoulders. "Girls. Fine beautiful girls who will look just like their mother. And I will love them all as I do her."

"And as she has come to love you," Jarla whispered.

His arms closed tightly around her. "That is a good thing, Mistress," he murmured. "Let us go home. Suddenly I am anxious to face the Tribunal."